7334

F
PUT

Putnam, Alice

Westering

$12.95

DATE		
MAY 8 1991		
JUN 18		
MAY 27 '92		
MAR 23 '93		

© THE BAKER & TAYLOR CO.

Also by Alice Putnam

The Spy Doll

The Whistling Swans

Westering

Alice Putnam

LODESTAR BOOKS
Dutton   New York

No character in this book is intended to represent
any actual person; all the incidents of the story are
entirely fictional in nature.

Copyright © 1990 by Alice Putnam

Library of Congress Cataloging-in-Publication Data

Putnam, Alice.
   Westering/Alice Putnam.—1st ed.
      p.   cm.
   "Lodestar books."
   Summary: Traveling with his family in a wagon train from Missouri
to Oregon in 1850, eleven-year-old Jason finds a stray dog
during the dangerous journey.
   ISBN 0-525-67299-0
   [1. Dogs—Fiction.   2. Overland journeys to the Pacific—Fiction.
3. Frontier and pioneer life—Fiction.   4. West (U.S.)—Fiction.]
I. Title.
PZ7.P9795We   1990   89-13238
[Fic]—dc20   CIP
                                                          AC

Published in the United States by Lodestar Books,
an affiliate of Dutton Children's Books,
a division of Penguin Books USA Inc.

Published simultaneously in Canada by
Fitzhenry & Whiteside Limited, Toronto

Editor: Rosemary Brosnan   Designer: Richard Granald/LMD

Printed in the U.S.A.   First Edition   10 9 8 7 6 5 4 3 2 1

For Jeffrey

They took to each other right from the start. It was as if they belonged together.

The dog wasn't much to look at, not big but not little, either. It was white with brown markings, and it had a tail that twisted to one side and a pair of floppy ears that were too big for the rest of its body. There was a furrow of worry between its eyes, which were very wise and very sad.

"Lost, are you?" Jason asked, holding out his hand.

The crooked tail began to wag. The mongrel inched toward him and, cringing a little, let him touch its matted fur.

"You'd best go home where you belong." Jason didn't really mean that. He didn't want the dog to go. Besides, it had no home—it was a stray, he could tell. There were plenty of them roaming the streets of Independence, abandoned by their owners. Folks had second thoughts about taking pets along, once they got to Missouri and were ready to start the trek across the prairie.

This dog wasn't like the others, though. It was different somehow, Jason thought. Not just because it had picked *him* out and followed him all the way down Main Street. No sir. It was smarter than most dogs. Anybody could see that. It seemed to know what he was thinking.

The dog sat down on the steps of the General Mercantile Store and waited while he went inside. The first thing Jason saw in the store was a row of candy jars on the counter that held peppermint sticks and licorice. Then he noticed the picture of Zachary Taylor, who was president now. "Old Rough and Ready" everybody called him. On the wall beside the picture was a calendar. May 10, 1850 it said. That was today, Jason's eleventh birthday. There wouldn't be any special celebration, though—not even a cake. His mother had told him that. Not with them leaving for Oregon tomorrow and so much to do to get ready. There wouldn't be any presents, either, because they had no money for such things.

The storekeeper came to the counter, snapping the elastic bands that held up his sleeves. Jason pointed to a nest of boxes. "Please . . . is there any mail for my pa, Henry Bartow?" he asked.

The storekeeper, who was also postmaster, turned to see. "Hmm. Bartow, you say?" Squinting, he sorted through the batch of envelopes, then shook his head. "Sorry, son. Nothing for you today. Later in the week, maybe."

"We'll be gone by then."

"That so?" The man leaned over, his long face closer to Jason's. "You one of them headin' west?"

Jason nodded. He looked again at the calendar. It showed a picture of two men straddling a creek, panning for gold. The storekeeper glanced at it, too, and smiled.

"Your pa aimin' to strike it rich out there in California like all the rest?"

"No, sir. We're going to Oregon. Ma, Pa, my sister and

me." Jason sighed. He couldn't help wishing they *were* bound for California. That would be a lot more exciting. But his father wasn't interested in gold. All he wanted was some of the land he'd heard was free for the taking, to set up a farm better than the one they'd just left in Pennsylvania.

"Well, thank you," he said, and went outside.

The dog was still there, wriggling a welcome. They walked on, the mongrel trotting at his heels.

Uneasy thoughts went round and round in Jason's head. Could he keep the dog? Would Pa allow him to? Even without asking him he knew the answer.

His father had bought them a covered wagon. It was clumsy and top-heavy, made of canvas and wood, with wheels of iron. He'd traded their farm horses for a double yoke of oxen to haul it. It was waiting right now, packed and ready, down by the river. Tomorrow they'd cross the Missouri, along with twenty other families who wanted to homestead in Oregon.

Under the floorboard of the wagon were stored sacks of provisions—flour, bacon, beans—enough to feed them for awhile, anyway. The rest of the space was stacked with what few belongings they could take. Jason thought of the tools, feather bedding, and pots and pans heaped against his mother's favorite rocking chair. Somewhere in the jumble, too, was the clock his great-grandfather had made in Germany. They couldn't leave that behind, not when it had been part of the family for so long. The clock had crossed the Atlantic Ocean with Jason's grandfather when he came to settle in Pennsylvania, before Jason's mother was born. It had been keeping time for them ever since. They couldn't leave behind the Bible either, which used to sit on top of the table in the parlor and held a record of when folks were born and died.

The wagon was crowded, all right. There was hardly room for his mother and his sister, Abbie, to sleep inside. As it was, he and Pa had to roll up in blankets underneath the wagon and trust that a bad storm wouldn't come up.

This dog, though . . . Jason looked at it thoughtfully. Those skinny legs could never keep up with the oxen for long. And Pa wouldn't hear of it taking up space, riding with them all. No chance of that. He'd best make a clean break right now.

"Look here," he said to the dog. He rammed his fists into the pockets of his pants. That way he wouldn't be tempted to pat the head turned up to him. "I like you. You and me, we could get along together fine. If I was to have a dog, you'd be the one I'd pick."

He'd never had a dog of his own. Oh, there was old Ben, who died last year, but he'd belonged to everybody, not just him. And Ben had been too busy keeping the cows and sheep in line to pay him much attention.

"But you can't go with me. Not where I'm goin'."

The mongrel nuzzled the sleeve of his homespun shirt.

Jason shook his fist. "Now you *git!*" he said, his voice so mean he almost scared himself. He took one last look at the dog's puzzled face, then quickly plunged into the heavy traffic of the street. A horse-drawn carriage missed him by inches. The driver yelled at him, but he kept on running, not glancing back at all. His heart was pounding.

He didn't halt even to catch his breath until he reached the muddy banks of the Missouri, where their wagon and the others stood. Over his shoulder he saw the dog still trailing him. It was panting in an effort to catch up with him, its ears flapping crazily, its paws flailing the air. "Oh, no!" he groaned.

His mother was bending over a fire near the wagon, skillet in hand, ready to start supper. Maybe if he asked her *she'd* say he could have the dog. Maybe she'd understand. By now the dog had caught up with him. He scooped it up in his arms and went to her. But before he could say anything his father came striding up from the river.

"What's that you've got?" He pushed his broad-rimmed hat back from his forehead. Jason could see the frown already forming there.

"He followed me, Pa. Back from town. He doesn't belong to anybody. He needs a home and he—"

"You know better'n to bring him here. What's got into you, boy? Don't you have any sense at all?"

Jason tightened his arms about the dog.

"But I thought . . ." He looked at his mother. "It's my birthday, remember? I know you said there'd be no presents, but if I could just have *him* . . ." He clutched the dog to him, felt its warm tongue lick his face.

His mother set the skillet aside and smoothed her apron. "It *is* his birthday, Henry," she said gently.

The frown on his father's face deepened. "You're as soft as the boy," he said. "A dog's the last thing we want right now."

"I'll take care of him, Pa. Honest," Jason begged. "He'll be no trouble."

"If I'm any judge, trouble is that mutt's middle name," his father said, snorting in disgust. "Get rid of him. I don't care how. Just do it. Right away."

Jason made one last mute appeal to his mother, but she was slicing potatoes into a pot as though everything were settled. He knew it would be no use arguing.

He took the dog, still nestled in his arms, up to where the main road curved away from the river and set him free. Then

5

he threw a stone at him, missing him on purpose. The mongrel, bewildered, raced after it, thinking it was a game. That was Jason's chance to get away. Back to their wagon he dashed. He scrambled up into it and hid behind a chest.

A few minutes later he heard the dog snuffling around outside, whining softly. He heard his father's voice, too, harsh with anger, and covered his ears to block out both sounds.

After awhile he uncovered his ears. His mother was calling him to supper. He climbed down from the wagon slowly, looking right and left. Part of him was afraid the dog would still be there; part of him was afraid it wouldn't be. There was no sign of it.

Well, that's that, he thought. Pa was probably right. Good riddance. What would I do with a dog like that, anyway?

He knew he ought to be glad, but he wasn't. Instead, there was a strange, empty feeling inside him. It was still there, gnawing at him like hunger, when he went to bed. He searched the darkness before crawling under the wagon and wrapping himself in his blanket. A small shadow moved in the bushes beyond the campfire, outlined by its fading embers. He stared at it hard. Was it . . . Could it be?

But no. It was only the east wind stirring some leaves. Sighing, he lay down on the hard ground. The dog was probably back in town by now, following somebody else— somebody who could give it a home. He'd never see it again.

He rubbed his eyes. Through the spokes of the wagon wheel he watched the far-away stars glimmering, splintered by a mist of tears.

2

Jason awoke early the next morning, long before anyone—even the sun—was up. The ground was hard and cold under his blanket. Not much like his bed back home in Pennsylvania. He shivered and drew his knees up to his chin. Then he lay still, watching the slow rise and fall of his father's breathing, trying not to toss and turn and rouse him. He sniffed the sour dampness of fog rising from the river.

The first thing that came to his mind was the dog. He missed him even more than last night. He could imagine how it would feel right now if they were sharing the blanket. With the dog's warm, furry body close to him, he wouldn't mind the cold at all.

Thinking like that was no good, though. All it did was push a knot up in his throat again. So he shut his eyes, trying to forget.

Today they'd cross the old Missouri. From what he'd heard the men say, it wasn't going to be easy. A ferry would carry them over, but it was nothing more than a couple of rickety flatboats tied together, drawn by a rope back and forth across

7

the river with pulleys. Only two wagons could go over at a time. The wheels had to be taken off, too. Jason had listened when Mr. McDermott explained why. If the wheels were left on, the wagons might start to roll when the ferry started. There'd be accidents. Folks might get hurt and maybe even drown. Or they could lose everything they owned. That's what McDermott said, and if he said it, it had to be right.

Jason was sure glad McDermott was in charge of their outfit, taking them to Oregon. He was gruff as a hungry bear just stirring from a winter's sleep. He even looked like one, with a grizzled beard covering most of his face and big, hairy hands, like paws. But he knew what he was about. Everyone in the train agreed on that. If anybody could get them past the Rockies safely it was Angus McDermott, they said. He'd been a mountain man, hunting and trapping in the west so long he could find the trail blindfolded, smelling the way.

"Get up, son." Jason felt Pa's hand clamp his shoulder and shake him. "You aim to sleep all day? There's work a'plenty for us both. We better start stirrin'."

Quickly, Jason scrambled from under the wagon and stretched, yawning. Other families were waking now. Fires for cooking were started and plumes of smoke rose, unfurling like banners in the early morning breeze. He breathed deeply, filling his lungs with the crisp air, then crossed his arms, slapping at the jacket he had worn all night. It was right brisk there by the river. Hard to believe it was May.

Someone yanked at his sleeve. He looked down and saw his sister Abbie's pert little face. Abbie, who came up to his elbow, was carrying a rag doll, the one with the yellow yarn braids Ma had made that looked just like her.

"Ma says you're to fetch some water. She says you're to hurry!"

Jason muttered to himself as he trotted off to get a bucket. Abbie liked to boss him around. To hear her, you'd never believe she was only five years old. He was thankful he had just one sister. That was enough. Most of the time he was able to ignore her, but today was different. Everybody was rushing around getting ready to leave and he was glad to be given some orders so he could be busy, too—even if it meant taking them from Abbie.

When he returned with the water, the bacon was frying and his mother had set out last night's biscuits. Soon a pot of coffee bubbled on the fire. Hastily, he and Pa drank some. It burned his mouth, and he fanned at his tongue as the two of them set off to tend to the stock. They didn't have much. Just the two yoke of oxen, the cow his mother insisted on taking along for milk, and Harry, Pa's gelding. Pa was right fond of that horse. He couldn't bring himself to sell it with the others.

"Howdy, Bartow." McDermott had caught up with them. He was wearing that wide, battered hat of his. Jason had never seen him without it. He always kept it pulled far down over his eyes, almost meeting the beard that grew up his cheeks. Jason wondered how he could see to get around at all. He stared at the hat. He sure wouldn't mind having one like it. It had a leather band trimmed with porcupine quills dyed red and yellow. In the middle of the band was stuck a drooping eagle's feather.

"You got that wagon of your'n set to move out?" McDermott loomed over them. He was even taller than Pa. A lot taller.

"Well, just about . . ." Jason's father hesitated. "The wife's

9

got some last minute packing." He scratched his chin. "You know how women are . . ."

The way McDermott scowled Jason didn't think he knew at all. He felt sorry for Pa.

"Thunderation, man!" The mountain guide seemed to grow two feet taller. His voice was so loud it made Jason's ears ring. "This ain't no tea party! That ferry's waitin' to load. When your turn comes up, you better be settin' there with all your gear, ready to shove off. That is, if you aim to travel with *my* outfit!"

McDermott sure sounded as though he meant it. He sounded as though all twenty-one wagons in the train going west belonged to him. He made it plenty clear, all right, who was in charge.

"Yes, *sir*. I'll hurry the missus along. Get on it right away." Pa's voice was meek, which was a real surprise to Jason. He'd never heard him answer anyone like that before. Pa had always been the one who was the boss.

"Takin' those wheels off will be a real chore," Pa told Jason as they walked away. "When it comes time to do it, I can use an extra pair of strong arms like yours."

Jason straightened his shoulders and puffed out his chest with pride. He took longer steps to match Pa's stride.

At last they had everything packed securely in the wagon. They drove it down to the river's edge. The wheels couldn't be removed until it was rolled aboard the ferry. There were two wagons ahead of them, so they would have to wait their turn.

The pair of flatboats shoved off, taking the first load across the river. Jason had been eager to get started, but now he looked warily at the rope that, with its system of pulleys, operated the ferry. It wasn't so thick, now that he saw it close up. Nor so tough, either. Supposing it broke halfway across the river? Supposing those flatboats went down under their heavy load? He shivered. Folks said the Missouri was plenty deep in some places.

He stood there on the bank, shifting from one foot to the other, his boots making a sucking sound in the mud. The sun slanted through the leaves of a willow. From the tree's branches came the rusty creak of a red-winged blackbird.

"Will we have to pay to go on the boat?" Abbie asked.

"Of course," Pa said. He jingled some coins in his pocket.

"Well, I just wish it was done and over with and we were safe on the other side," said Jason's mother, tightening the strings of her sunbonnet.

Suddenly everyone who was watching gasped! The ferry was dipping and bobbing in the swift current of the river. Water rushed over it, splashing the wagons that had been lashed down. The women and children on board screamed.

But then the ferry steadied and moved on, finally reaching the opposite shore. When it returned for the next load, Jason hurried to help his father with their own wagon. Then he stood back while some of the men, grunting and pushing, got it on the ferry.

"What can I do now, Pa?" Jason asked when the wheels were off the wagon.

"Hold onto these ornery critters for me, son." Pa was struggling to fasten ropes around the horns of their lead ox. The flatboats couldn't carry livestock, so all the animals in the wagon train would have to swim across the river. The oxen were scared. They kept pulling back, tossing their heads and rolling their eyes until only the whites showed. Jason threw his arms around their necks and did his best to quiet them. He talked to them slow and easy, smoothing their flanks.

11

When the lead ox was finally roped, Pa mounted Harry, his gelding, and rode into the river. He tried to coax the livestock to follow. They braced their legs stubbornly, refusing to budge, until Jason grabbed a willow branch and whacked at their rumps. Then they stepped cautiously into the water, bellowing so loud Jason was sure folks must hear them clear back on Main Street.

"All right, Jason!" Pa called. "Now you'd best get yourself aboard!"

"Yes! Hurry! You'll be left behind!" Ma's blue sunbonnet poked around the side of their wagon. She and Abbie were already settled on the ferry.

Jason took a quick look around to make sure they had everything that belonged to them. Then he sprinted through the shallow water, grabbed for the edge of the flatboat, and swung himself up. He slumped against the warm wood and closed his eyes against the sun's glare, feeling the boat move away from shore.

When he opened his eyes again he saw a small shape on the bank of the river, running back and forth in a frantic kind of way. A shrill bark echoed across the water.

The dog again! It hadn't forgotten him! It still wanted to be with him, to go wherever he was going. The bond between them was too strong to be broken, Jason realized. The dog knew it and so did he.

Jason looked back at Pa, too busy with the oxen to notice anything else. What if I was to go against him, Jason asked himself. What if I was to swim back for the dog and . . .

Just then the dog plunged into the water and began paddling to him. It rose and sank. Come on! Jason urged silently.

One final spurt and thrashing and the dog was close enough to reach. He swept up the wet and quivering dog and

12

held it in his arms. He thought it would never stop licking his face, it was that glad to see him.

"Nobody's going to keep us apart, you an' me, from now on," he promised. The dog listened, its face upturned. "You hear? Nobody!"

He told himself Pa surely wouldn't make him turn the dog loose on the other side of the river. There were no houses or people there, nothing but wild country. This time Pa would *have* to let him keep it. Wouldn't he?

Jason hid the dog under his jacket, hoping Ma hadn't seen it. She had, though. Nothing much got past those quick eyes of hers.

"Come here, Jason," she called. She leaned out of their wagon. "What's that you have?" The dog poked its head from Jason's jacket and she reared back in surprise. "Mercy! It's that stray again! Looks half drowned, poor thing." She patted its dripping fur gingerly. "It's right pitiful. Where on earth did it come from?"

"It swam the river to get to us, Ma. We *got* to keep it now, don't we?"

"Well, I don't know about that. Your Pa . . ."

"Pa's gonna be real mad when he sees that dog!" Abbie's shrill little voice broke in. "Just you wait," she told Jason, her blue eyes bright as two buttons. "*You're* gonna catch it!"

Jason stared out at the river. She was probably right, he thought glumly. Now he wasn't at all anxious to get to shore. It meant he'd have to face up to Pa and do some hard explaining. Maybe argue some, too. Although that hardly ever worked.

Pa, mounted on Harry, wasn't far behind the ferry now. He was yanking at the rope tied around the horns of the lead ox, a stubborn beast, determined to turn back to shore. Suddenly, Jason saw the ox give a mighty jerk. The rope snapped and broke. The ox started to drift downstream, floundering against the current. The other oxen all panicked, churning the water, drifting off, too.

"Ho . . . eee . . . eee!" Pa yelled. He spun Harry around and went after them. Some of the men on shore leaped onto their horses and came to help. The lead ox reared up for a second, then his big head disappeared under the water. He's a goner! Jason thought. But then Pa reached down and gave a yank. He pulled the beast's head up, grabbed the broken end of rope, and towed the ox along.

Soon after that, the ferry landed, and they all got off. Jason kept the dog hidden under his jacket, waiting for Pa. As soon as he saw him, Jason knew he was in a bad mood. No wonder. He was soaked to the skin. He'd lost his hat and he was scowling, muttering to himself. This was no time to show him the dog, Jason knew. He'd have to keep him out of sight until Pa simmered down. But where could he hide him?

Inside their wagon, near the back, was a pile of Ma's quilts. He put the dog there. To be on the safe side, he tied him to the handle of a chest.

"Now you be still, hear?" He pointed a finger. "Lie down." The dog did as he was told.

Next Jason cornered Abbie, playing blindman's buff with some other children. "Mind you don't say a word to Pa about that dog," he said. "I aim to tell him myself when I'm good

15

an' ready." Which wouldn't be for awhile, because Pa was helping the others by bringing more cattle over.

At last everyone was across the river. While the women fixed something to eat, the men stretched out on the ground to rest. Not McDermott, though. Jason watched him go around, thumping the water barrels lashed to the sides of the wagons to make sure they were full before starting out again. He checked the tar buckets, too. Every wagon had one hanging from its axle. The buckets were filled half with tar and half with tallow, and were needed to keep the iron wheels of the wagons greased and rolling smoothly.

When he came to their wagon, McDermott bellowed, "Bartow! Look here! The way you got this tied on it won't last more'n a mile!"

Pa rose to his feet wearily. He and McDermott bent over the tar bucket. Jason felt every muscle tighten. They were mighty close to where the dog was. If he barked now . . .

Just then a mournful howl came from the wagon.

Jason stiffened. Pa and McDermott looked at him.

"What was *that*?" asked Pa.

"Sounded like a dog to me," said McDermott. "A mighty unhappy one, at that."

Pa stared at Jason, his face grim. "If it's that mutt again . . ." he said. "Fetch him! Right now!"

Jason brought the dog out. He was squirming, trying to get free to run. McDermott reached over and patted him with a big calloused hand. "Belong to you, does he?" he asked Jason.

"Well . . . kind of . . ." Jason stammered. "I mean, he . . ."

Pa turned on Jason angrily. "Thought I told you to run that critter off back in Independence! What's he doin' here? You

16

sneaked him over the river, didn't you? Don't tell me you didn't! Why, I ought to take my belt an'—"

"Hold on, now!" McDermott stepped between them. "No cause to get riled up. Just because we got no other dogs in this outfit don't mean he ain't welcome." He curled his fingers about the dog's jaw. "This here's a right sassy li'l feller. Got huntin' blood in him, too. Wouldn't surprise me none if he turned out to be a fair coon hound."

"Honest?" Jason began to feel better. If the mountain man took a liking to him maybe Pa would, too.

"Yessir. I had a hound like this once." McDermott inspected the animal's teeth. "Called him Scout."

"That's what I'll name *this* one," Jason answered, pleased.

"No need to name him," Pa said curtly. "He's not going to be around that long."

"But, Pa . . ."

McDermott thrust his bearded face close to Pa. "What d'you plan to do with him, Bartow? You can't turn him loose here." His arm swept the barren land. "Not unless you're a heap meaner than I figger." His eyes glinted like bits of bright metal.

Pa still scowled. "But look at him! That runt could never keep up with the oxen. And as for carryin' him in the wagon . . ."

"I can hold him, Pa! He's not a bit heavy. And he'd be still. You'd hardly know he was around at all."

"The boy's right." McDermott nodded, then reached out and scratched the dog behind the ear. "No problem a'tall, far as I can see." He turned to Jason. "You got yourself a fine hound. Train him right. Don't let him make a nuisance of hisself." He winked and walked off.

17

Jason hugged the dog. McDermott wasn't such a hard man as folks said.

After he was gone, though, Pa tore into Jason. "What riles me most is you sneakin' that cur here after what I told you. Bringin' him clear across the river—"

"But I didn't bring him, Pa! He started swimmin' out to me and—"

His father held up his hand to silence him. "I don't want to hear any more of your pack of lies. It's done now. We'll have to make the best of it. For awhile, anyway."

Jason swallowed hard, then asked, "What do you mean, for awhile?"

"I mean you can keep him until we get to Fort Laramie. No longer. We'll rid ourselves of him thére. Someone at the post will likely take him."

Fort Laramie. The next real stopping place on the trail west. Jason had heard McDermott say they could make it there in about forty days, barring accidents and unseen delays. He could keep Scout for only a little more than a month. Then he'd have to give him up for good.

He took out his pocket knife. He kept the blade real sharp. With it, he made a notch in the wood of the wagon's side. He aimed to mark off every day. That way he could keep track of the time. A lot could happen in forty days. Why, Pa might even take a liking to Scout. That was what Jason told himself, not much believing it.

4

The wagon train made only a few miles that day, then halted for the night. Next morning, though, they were off to an early start. The first rays of the rising sun glinted against McDermott's horse, making its mane shine like copper. "Ride out!" McDermott yelled, whipping off his broad-brimmed hat and swinging it above his head like a banner. "Let 'er roll!"

Everybody else yelled, too—Jason louder than anyone—as the wagons began to move. They were sure enough heading West now!

The creaking wheels sounded like a swarm of giant insects winging along the trail. Jason's father clicked his tongue against his teeth and shouted "Haw!" His long whip curled across the rump of the lead ox.

The wagon started its swaying motion. Harry, Pa's horse, trotted along, tied to the back. Ma and Abbie rode inside, but Jason sat on the seat next to Pa. He braced Scout against his stomach. He could feel him quivering—Scout was almost as excited as *he* was.

They both stared out at the prairie all around them. Miles

and miles of flat land, far as the eye could see. Nothing but waist-high grass, rippling in the wind.

The wheels jolted against a rut and Jason held Scout tighter. A lot of other wagons had come this way before, and had made a kind of path for them to follow. Just the same, Jason was glad McDermott was up there ahead. He knew which way to go.

After awhile Abbie began to fuss, and Ma let her climb on the seat beside Jason. Scout licked her face and she giggled.

"Scout's a silly name, isn't it, Pa?" she said.

"It is for *that* mutt." Pa glanced at the dog and gave a little snort. "Why, I reckon he couldn't as much as find his way out of a barn. Not unless he was pointed in the right direction."

Pa and Abbie both had a good laugh over that. But Ma called out from within the wagon, "Well, you notice he found *Jason* all right!" Jason turned around and smiled at her gratefully.

At nooning the wagon train stopped to rest and let the livestock graze. Ma took out some sourdough bread and cut a few slices of ham, but Jason didn't want to eat with his family. He might have to listen to more of Pa and Abbie's joshing. "I'm gonna let Scout stretch his legs," he said.

Ma gave him his share of the food. "Now mind you keep most of that for yourself," she said. "Don't feed it all to the dog. There'll be no coming back for seconds. We've got to be careful and make our supplies last."

Jason ran off, with the dog bounding at his heels. They sat down behind a mound of bunchgrass where his folks couldn't see them and divided the food. Scout took his share real polite-like, not even snatching.

After they had eaten, Jason stretched out, with Scout at his side. He threw one arm across the dog. It felt good, lying

20

there in the warm grass that smelled sweet as new-cut hay. He could hear some of the other children playing not far off, but he was glad to be right where he was.

Just then he saw someone coming. Luke, the oldest Watson boy. He was about Jason's age but they weren't exactly friends.

Luke threw himself down beside Jason, breathing hard as if he'd been in a race. "That Run Sheep Run is fun for little kids but I got better things to do," he said. "My pa lets me tend our cows. We got six, one nearly ready to calve. They take a heap of lookin' after." He chewed on a blade of grass. "You got any cattle?"

"Just our milk cow." Jason thought of the churn that swung from the rear of their wagon. When they poured some of the milk into the churn, the motion of the jogging wagon turned the cream to butter.

"This your dog?" Luke reached out, but Scout bared his teeth. Scout doesn't want him for a friend, either, Jason thought.

"Wonder how he is with cattle," Luke said. Jason looked at the cows grazing nearby. They were free to roam, not tethered like the horses.

"I dunno," he said. There were a lot of things about Scout he didn't know.

"Likely he couldn't make 'em mind," said Luke. He took off his hat, a round one with a big brim, and slapped at Scout, teasing.

Before Jason knew what was happening, Scout had the hat in his mouth and was off, headed straight for the cattle. He dashed in and out between their legs, barking. The cows bawled and kicked at him and one old bull chased him, snorting and tossing his horns. The next thing Jason knew the whole herd was thundering off in all directions.

21

Luke jumped to his feet. "He's spooked 'em!" He raced after them, yelling "Whoa-ee-ee!"

The men came running. A couple of them hurriedly saddled horses and went galloping after the stampeding cattle. They whooped and hollered, trying to round up the herd. After awhile they were back, driving the cows ahead of them. Mr. Watson, Luke's father, started to count. "I'm missin' one," he said. "A two-year-old. Best heifer of the lot. She scares easy. Must be hidin' out somewhere."

Jason could hear McDermott mutter something about "greenhorns" who didn't know any better than to try to fetch a lot of cows along, crossing the Rockies.

"What started all the ruckus, anyway?" Jason's father asked.

"That mutt!" Luke pointed to Scout, who was panting, his tongue hanging, his sides heaving. "Him an' his fool barkin' . . ."

"You got him riled, that's why—" Jason started to say.

Pa cut him short. "That's enough out of you, boy!"

"About my heifer . . ." Mr. Watson whined.

"Forget her," snapped McDermott. "We've wasted enough time already. I aim to move out in two shakes of a lamb's tail."

Mr. Watson turned to Pa. "You'll pay for that cow!" He shook his fist in Pa's face. "Twenty-five dollars she's worth. That's what two-year-olds were bringin' back in Independence. You'll pay me or—"

"Or *what*?" Pa thrust out his jaw.

"Hold on there!" McDermott stepped between them. "I reckon you'll have to pay, Bartow. But twenty-five dollars is a mite steep, to my way of thinkin'. Fifteen is more likely."

"Fifteen!" Watson sputtered. "Why, I'm bein' robbed! In Independence—"

"I don't give a dang about Independence, man! We're on

22

the plains now." McDermott spat on the ground. "Take it or leave it."

Pa put his hands in his pockets. "I don't carry cash with me. But c'mon to the wagon. I'll settle." He strode off, Watson trailing behind him.

When they were gone, McDermott laid a heavy hand on Jason's shoulder. "Boy, I thought I told you to watch out for that dog, see he don't cause trouble. Maybe you didn't hear me right?"

Jason's throat went dry. He swallowed hard. "Yessir, I heard."

"Wal, you're hearin' me again." McDermott's eyes were like gray ice, making Jason almost shiver. "He gets to be a pest an' he's done for. That spelled out plain enough?"

"Yessir," Jason said again. No use trying to explain to McDermott how it all started. He wouldn't listen anymore than Pa would. Jason dragged his feet going back to the wagon. He looked at Scout. The dog seemed to know he'd done wrong. His tail was between his legs and his ears drooped more than ever. The wrinkled fold of worry was back between his eyes.

"See what you did? Made McDermott mad. And now Pa hates you for sure."

Scout whimpered and Jason couldn't help but comfort him. Rubbing the dog's head made Jason feel better. But not much.

23

5

Jason's father wasn't about to let him forget what had happened.

"Fifteen dollars I had to pay Watson for his cow!" He bit off the words angrily. "All on account of that stray mutt!" He scowled at Scout, who whined and hung his head. "I told you he'd bring us nothin' but trouble. You've not had him more'n a day and he's started already."

"Don't blame Scout, Pa." Jason had to speak up, even though he knew it wouldn't do any good. "Most dogs would have done the same thing he did. The way Luke was teasin' him—"

"Well, for two cents I'd dump him right here and now."

"Pa! You wouldn't!" Jason caught his breath. He searched his father's face. Did he mean what he'd just said?

"Don't torment the boy, Henry." His mother reached out from the wagon and touched his father's arm. "You know you'd do no such thing."

"I sure enough feel like it!" Pa turned to Jason, his face as dark as a thundercloud. "Now get this straight, son. That

24

critter causes us any more worry an' he's *never* goin' to see Fort Laramie."

Jason nodded his head and didn't say another word. He thought plenty, though.

More days passed. Hard days of getting up before it was light. Each morning the grass was wet with dew as Jason helped Pa tend their stock, and a chill wind blew across the prairie, making him glad to get back to the fire and breakfast.

As the wagon set out every morning, tossing from side to side, he felt as if he were on a ship. He'd never been on one but he'd read stories about the sea, so he knew what it must be like. He would look back at the long line of other wagons curving behind and imagine that their white tops were sails.

Often, as dawn streaked the sky with pink and gold, small wild creatures would spring up in the weeds beside the trail— rabbits and prairie hens surprised by the rumble of wheels.

Abbie complained a lot, especially when the wagon jolted through deep ruts. "I don't feel good, Ma," she would say, holding her stomach. "I feel sick." Ma would untie Abbie's sunbonnet and take it off, smoothing her hair. "There," she would say, "is that better?"

Jason didn't mind how much the wagon bumped and bounced. He pretended he was driving their team of oxen. "Haw!" he said to himself, and "Gee!" He made believe he was turning them left and right, and curling the whip above their flanks like Pa did.

Once in awhile he begged Pa to let him ride Harry. The horse got restless, tied to the back of the wagon. "I can handle him. Honest," Jason would plead. After all, hadn't he known Harry since he was a colt? He'd spent many an hour on his back, without a saddle even. Pa usually gave in. "Well, mind you keep him to an easy trot," he would say.

25

One day McDermott came by on his sorrel when Jason was riding Harry. The mountain man touched the brim of his hat in a mock salute. "You ought to be in the U.S. cavalry, boy," he said with a wink. He was fooling, but still it made Jason feel good.

At midday the train always stopped for nooning—a bite to eat and rest for folks and livestock. Jason was extra careful now to keep Scout from the grazing herd. He tried to stay clear of Luke Watson, too, but that wasn't easy. Luke seemed to want to hunt him out and taunt him. "Still got that runt of yours?" Luke would holler, so that folks couldn't help but hear. "Has he run off any cattle lately?" It made Jason mad, but he didn't answer. He didn't want more trouble with the Watsons, if he could help it.

Afternoons got tiresome. By then, the oxen plodded along, their splay feet hardly lifting at all. Pa nodded, his chin on his chest, rousing now and then to slap at them with the reins. The prairie was such a bright green it made Jason's eyes ache. He yawned, wishing he could take a nap on the feather mattress in the wagon like Ma and Abbie. Even Scout slept, his nose between his paws. Sometimes—not often—Jason dozed off in spite of himself. Then he jerked awake and reached for Scout to make sure he was still there.

McDermott always called a halt before sundown. He wanted to set up camp while there was still plenty of light. He always found them a place, too, with water. Jason wondered how he did it. They might have to go a few miles off the trail, but soon, sure enough, they'd come to a stream with maybe a few trees. The livestock could hardly wait to wade in. They drank as if they'd never get their fill.

"Fetch us some water, too," Ma would say, handing Jason their wooden pail. Then the work began for real. He had to

26

gather wood for the fire and help take off the yokes from the oxen. He had to rub down Harry and tether him where he could eat sweet grass. And, just when he was busiest, his mother would call, "Look after Abbie while I fix supper."

Supper was sure worth waiting for. Bread had been rising all day in the wagon, and now Ma baked it in an iron pot over the fire. It gave out a yeasty smell that made Jason lick his lips. Salt pork browned to crispness in the frying pan with iron legs that his mother called a "spider." Beans, thick with molasses, simmered in another pot. Each family prepared its own meal, and the delicious aromas mingled in the air. Jason went around sniffing them all. So did Scout. He stuck out his tongue as if he could taste the food.

When supper was ready, Ma ladled it, steaming, onto their tin plates. They all bowed their heads while Pa said grace. Then they ate hungrily. There was barely enough for each of them, and no second helpings. As Ma kept saying, their supplies had to last until they got to Fort Laramie. Pa seemed to watch every bite Jason fed Scout. He didn't say anything, though. And Ma always gave the dog scraps she purposely left in the pot.

At twilight, before it grew completely dark, the men drove the livestock into a corral outside the circle of wagons. McDermott showed them how to make it with chains and stakes and the yokes of the oxen. Every night he picked men to stand guard over the corral with rifles.

"We're in Indian territory now," he said. "Them Pawnee been follerin' us for some spell."

"They have been?" Jason's eyes widened. He hadn't seen any Indians. He quickly looked behind him, almost expecting to find one standing there.

"Yessir." McDermott's lips twitched as though something

had struck him funny. "Wouldn't surprise me none if they was to pay us a visit some night soon."

"What . . . for?" Jason stammered.

"Wal, not to say 'Howdy', exactly. More'n likely they got ideas 'bout our horses." He swung his arm in the direction of the corral.

"You mean . . . they want to *steal* them?"

McDermott's lips twitched again. "You might put it that way. Pawnees don't call it stealin', though. Helpin' themselves to any horses handy jist comes natural to 'em, 'specially when the horses is on their land." He was suddenly serious. "This *is* their land, boy. They was here first an' don't you forget it."

Jason thought about that for a minute. No wonder the Indians weren't too friendly. He wished there was some way the folks in the wagon train could talk to them and explain they meant no harm. Then nobody would need to be afraid.

"I've known some mighty fine Indians in my time," McDermott said. "Fact is, I'd be dead today if one tribe hadn't taken me in when I was starved an' half froze."

Jason thought about that, too. Then he said, "Well, maybe they won't come around with Scout here." Scout thumped his tail at the sound of his name. "He'd sure scare *anyone* off. He can bark louder'n a dog twice his size."

"I don't doubt that none." The mountain man knelt down and scratched Scout behind one ear. "Yessir, I reckon we're safe with *him* to watch out for us." He laughed. Jason didn't know why. He decided grown-ups were hard to understand sometimes.

At night, after the smaller children had been put to bed, the fun always began. Jason was allowed to stay up and watch if he kept quiet and was no bother.

28

Only one big campfire blazed now, throwing a light that flickered against the canvas of the circle of wagons. Sometimes Jason thought he could see moving figures behind the wagons, but they faded away as he looked at them. Were they Pawnees, he wondered? He felt uneasy and put his arm around Scout. If there *were* Indians on the prowl, Scout would be the first to know.

An old man with a white beard and shaky knees came over to the fire. He took out a fiddle, scraped it with a bow once or twice, then started a lively tune. Everybody clapped their hands in time to the music. Some of the men stamped their feet. "Skip-to-ma-Lou, my darlin'," they all sang.

The grown-ups began to dance. First the young, pretty girls were picked as partners and whirled around until their skirts flew up and their muslin petticoats showed. Then the shy, more homely ones had their turn, and the older folks joined in—even Jason's parents. Jason liked to watch them. Ma looked flushed and happy, the combs that held her hair slipping as she danced so that she had to keep pushing them in place. Pa wasn't as grim as he usually was, either. He laughed as he spun her around. He'd been tired earlier, when Jason helped him with the chores. Now he was as frisky as any of them.

McDermott didn't do any dancing. Instead, he sat by one of the wagons with his back braced against it, spinning tales for anyone who cared to listen. Jason always got as close to him as he could, not wanting to miss a word.

McDermott could tell some wonderful stories, all right. Some folks doubted whether they were true or not, but Jason didn't. He believed every word.

"Did I ever mention how I come to lose this here ear of mine?" McDermott asked one night. He took off his hat and shoved back his long hair. There was a jagged scar where his ear should have been. Jason gasped.

"I reckon I didn't." The mountain man gazed at the fire. "Wal, it was a grizzly done it. She had cubs, y'see, which made her ornery an' mean as all get out. I never figgered to tangle with her. I ain't *that* kind of fool. But she seen me afore I seen her an' . . ."

"And what?" came a chorus of voices.

"And afore I knowed what was happenin', she was onto me, rippin' an' slashin' an' howlin' like a hundred banshee. Them claws of hers was like knives. They dang near scalped me . . ." He drew a line across his head from one side to the other.

"I'd a been done fer, sure enough, but fer that pardner of mine. He come runnin' with his rifle, pumped her full of lead—"

Just then a shrill howl split the air. Again and again. Louder and louder. The music stopped. Everyone stood still, listening.

"Why, that's Scout!" Jason cried. He groped around for him. He had been lying at his feet a minute ago. Now he was gone.

6

"That dog's onto somethin'!" McDermott said, jumping up. He reached for the pistol slung in a leather holster low on his hips. "Over yonder by the corral!"

"Is it . . . Pawnee? Come to steal our horses?" Jason whispered. A ripple of fear swept over him. He tried to see past the wagons, but it was too dark.

The horses in the corral started to whinny. Scout was howling louder than ever now.

"You women folk—git to the wagons with your young uns, quick! Men—grab your rifles an' take cover! Don't fire less'n I give the word!" McDermott started for the corral at a fast lope, the moccasins he wore around camp not making a sound.

Jason tried to follow him but McDermott ordered, "Git back there with the rest! You want an arrow through your skull?"

Jason didn't have to be told twice. He ducked behind a barrel and crouched there, too scared almost to breathe.

Crack! A log on the fire split suddenly, sending sparks

31

flying all around. Jason's heart pounded so loud it made the blood beat against his ears like a drum. For just a second, in the burst of light, he thought he saw a face, out where the horses were, out where McDermott was heading. A face with *red skin*!

McDermott had disappeared now. Jason glanced around at the other men. They were kneeling behind the wagons, guns cocked and ready, waiting for the mountain man to give them the order to start shooting. Jason waited, too, every inch of him taut as the strings on the old man's fiddle.

For a few seconds nothing happened. Then, just about the time Jason figured McDermott had reached the corral, Scout quit howling. Everything was deadly still.

Now Jason was worried, sure enough. McDermott was sharp. He knew all about Indians, what they might do. But maybe these Pawnee were too sly even for him. They were bound to carry knives. What if they'd sneaked up behind him? Killed him, and Scout, too?

He stood up, forgetting what the mountain man had told him about staying covered, and started to run for the corral. He had to find out for himself. He couldn't just set there, not knowing.

Just as he reached the other side of the wagons something grabbed him in the darkness. It shook him so hard it made his teeth chatter.

"Don't you *never* mind what you're told, boy?"

Jason didn't have to see his face to know it was McDermott. He sounded plenty mad.

"One of these days you're gonna be mighty sorry if you keep on the way you're goin'. Fact is, you ain't gonna *live* long. Not in these parts, you ain't."

"I had to see if you were all right. I had to see if Scout . . ."

Scout was leaping at Jason's legs, carrying on as if they'd been apart a year or more.

McDermott yelled, "You folks—come on out now! No cause to be afeard!"

The women and children scurried from the wagons. Some of the little ones were crying, while the women, chattering, asked a heap of questions. The men crowded around McDermott, relief showing on their faces.

"Was it Pawnee? Are they gone? Did they get any of the horses?"

Everyone was talking at once and nobody was listening. Watson was swinging his rifle, shouting, "Which way did you say they went?", until McDermott took the gun from him, muttering, "Gimme that afore you shoot somebody. *Yerself,* most likely."

"Was there Indians out there, for a fact?" someone asked in a loud voice. Before McDermott could answer, Luke broke in. "Naw. It was just that blame dog again, stirrin' up a ruckus, for nothin'." He looked straight at Jason and sneered, as if daring him to say it wasn't so.

"Can't say for certain." McDermott sounded calm and steady. "I checked the corral. No livestock missin'. I'll have another look around in the morning, soon's it gets light. Might come onto some tracks." He took off his hat and wiped the inside band of it with his sleeve. "One thing sure—if it *was* Pawnee they won't be back again. Not tonight. We kin all go to bed now an' sleep sound."

On the way to the wagons, Luke bumped against Jason. He did it on purpose, Jason knew. "That dog of yours—he sure keeps things lively, don't he?" He nudged Jason hard in the ribs. "You can't tell *me* he was onto Indians. Nobody else thinks so, either."

33

Jason didn't answer. He was sure—well, almost sure—Scout had warned them of real danger. He remembered the face he had seen, red in the firelight. Had it been real? Or had he just imagined it was there?

The next day Jason knew for certain he'd been wrong about Scout and the Pawnee. Two things happened to make him sure. First off, McDermott told him he could find no trace of Indians. "But that don't mean they wasn't there," he said. He didn't sound as if he believed it, though, and Jason didn't, either.

Then Pa took it into his head he wanted Scout with him that night when he made his rounds. It was Pa's turn to stand guard duty. He and Ira Wilson had to patrol the campsite for four hours while other folks slept. At midnight they would be relieved by two other men and could go to bed themselves. That was the way McDermott had figured it all out—fair, like everything he did.

"Might not be a bad idea if that dog of yours was to keep watch with me and Ira," Pa said. "Wilson's a mite hard of hearing and we could do with an extra pair of sharp ears." He gave Scout a glance that was almost friendly.

Jason was pleased. That must mean Pa was beginning to like the dog. He must think he was of some use after all. He grinned as his father and Scout went off together. Then he rolled up in his blanket and went to sleep.

A few hours later, though, he was jarred awake. What was that sound he heard? Scout! Not just barking. Howling almost as loud as the wolves that sometimes called to each other across the plains. It was a mournful sound that sent chills down his spine.

Everyone was awake now. Folks came crawling out of the wagons, rubbing their eyes. Men grabbed up their rifles and

34

went running. Jason ran, too, hitching at his pants, his bare feet cold against the ground.

When he got to where Scout was, Pa and McDermott were there. Scout had stopped his howling. He was hanging his head, looking shamed.

"What's up? What's the matter?" everyone was asking, clustering around.

Pa didn't answer. He just glared at Scout. Jason could see a muscle in Pa's cheek twitching the way it did when he was real upset.

"It's all right, folks. No cause for alarm." McDermott herded people back toward their wagons. "Didn't you never hear a hound before, bayin' at the moon?" He pointed to the huge yellow sphere that hung in the sky. "Couldn't blame him much. Not when it's the size of that un."

Everyone went away, muttering. Jason slid back in the shadows, hoping no one would see him. He was even more ashamed than Scout was—and worried, too, about what folks would think, being stirred up a second time like that for no reason.

"Jason! Go on to bed!"

Pa had seen him, then.

"An' take this mutt of yours with you." His words stung like a whip.

McDermott didn't say anything. But Jason could feel the mountain man's eyes following him as he started back to the wagon.

35

7

"McDermott's called a council meeting for tonight," Jason's father said the next day.

"Oh? What for?" Ma glanced up from brushing Abbie's long blonde hair and plaiting it in two braids.

"Can't say." Pa scratched the stubble of his beard. He looked hard at Jason, and Jason flinched. Was the meeting about Scout, he wondered? Was McDermott going to say they should get rid of him?

"It must be important," Ma said. "Mr. McDermott doesn't call you men together unless it is. I remember the last time—it was to tell you supplies were low. He warned we'd have to be more saving of them."

"Well, I have a notion tonight he means to settle that fuss with Sam Morgan. Him and the bullwacker—you know, the feller who signed on to help with his oxen," Pa said. "Among *other* things." He looked at Jason again.

"Too bad those two can't get along." Jason's mother said with a sigh. "Why, I heard Mr. Morgan actually shot the bullwacker in the leg. Just over a game of cards!"

"That's not how it happened, exactly. It was an accident, pure an' simple. Sam never meant to harm the bullwacker. They got to arguin' and Sam's rifle went off. Hit the feller in the foot. Now he's goin' around limpin' and tellin' folks he figgers to get even."

Ma's hand flew to her mouth. "Mercy! I hope he doesn't!" She smoothed her calico dress, then tied on a fresh apron. "It's a wonder we don't have more real quarrels. Everybody's getting so tired and quick-tempered."

"Well, I know one feller who'd best keep out of my way, if he knows what's good for him, and that's Watson." Pa flushed darkly. "He was hecklin' me again this morning about that dog of Jason's." His hand clenched into a tight fist. "One of these days I'm gonna have to shut him up!"

"Now, Henry, don't talk like that! You're such a hot-head yourself sometimes." She touched his sleeve gently. "Promise me you won't get in a fight with Mr. Watson. *Promise*."

"If I do, Watson won't come out the winner, I'll say that much." He slapped his hat on his head and left.

That evening Jason's mother took Abbie and went to visit with a friend who had just had a baby a week ago. Women didn't attend the council meetings. Their husbands told them what was discussed there. Children weren't supposed to go to the meetings, either. Jason knew that. He had to go, though. He had to be there in case they talked about Scout.

As soon as his parents left the wagon, he slipped away, taking Scout with him. They both hid in the shadows near the camp fire. Jason put one arm around the dog, to make certain he'd be still.

The men were already gathered around the fire, listening to what McDermott was saying. One of them tossed on another log, and sparks, like tiny stars in the darkness, flew up with a sputtering sound.

"So that's how it is," McDermott declared, crossing his arms on his chest. Jason could see the light from the flames flicker on his beard. "There'll be no more feudin' between you two. You got that through your thick heads?" He pointed to a couple of men sitting on opposite sides of the fire. Jason recognized them as the ones Pa had talked about. One man—the bullwacker—wasn't wearing a boot and had a strip of cloth tied about his foot. He'd been shot, all right.

"Shake hands on it, then," McDermott ordered. They did as they were told, heads down, not in any hurry.

The mountain man nodded. "Now, we got somethin' more important than this danged fightin' amongst ourselves to take care of."

Jason held his breath. What was it? Was he going to talk about Scout now?

McDermott cleared his throat. It sounded like a bullfrog's croak. "Mebbe you don't know it, but we'll be gittin' to the Platte tomorrow. That's one sneaky river, I want to tell you. It don't look like much. Only about a mile wide where we'll be crossin'. Water so durn muddy folks say you got to chew it, 'stead of drink it. But don't let that give you the notion it's tame. It ain't. It's a bed of quicksand."

"How can we cross the dang thing, then?" a man by the name of Johnson asked. He shifted a wad of tobacco in his mouth and spat into the fire. "There's no ferry in these parts. Not lessn' it's run by Indians!" Everybody laughed at that.

"Wouldn't do us no good if there *was* a ferry," said McDermott. "River's too shallow most places." He stared at the faces turned up to him, then said, "Yes, sir. This is one time we better keep our wits about us. Lessn' we want the ole Platte to suck us in—wagons, stock, an' all.'"

Jason shivered, and not because a cool breeze was blowing, either. The Missouri had been scary enough. Now this river sounded even more dangerous.

"Seems to me we don't stand much chance." One man, who had been whittling a piece of wood, put down his knife.

"We do if we use our noggins." The mountain man paced back and forth, taking big strides. "I aim to go across ahead of the rest of you and sound that ole river out. I been over it afore plenty of times, but that don't mean a thing. The Platte's always changin'. I kin mark the way to take. Then you come after."

"How do you aim to mark it?" a fat man asked.

"With willow sticks. Like I say, the Platte's mighty shallow. Sandy bed. But findin' the safe spots in it is a mite risky." He hesitated a moment. "I'm gonna need another feller to help. Any volunteers?"

Everyone was silent. Then Jason's father raised his hand. "You can count me in, Mac," he said.

Jason looked at Pa, pride shining in his eyes. If he reached far enough, he could almost touch Pa's back. He wanted to, bad enough, but he didn't.

That settled, McDermott gave advice on how to handle the wagons and teams crossing the river. When he finished, everyone rose to leave.

"Just a minute . . ." It was Watson, sticking out his chest, trying to look important. He snapped his suspenders. "I got one more thing to bring up, seein' as we're all here. That mutt the Bartow kid has." He stared straight at Jason's father. "I vote we get rid of it. Now. I've had enough of its yappin' an' I reckon you have, too. It's already lost me a good milk cow an' two nights' sleep. Next time it'll bring the Pawnee down on us."

"How d'you figger that?" Pa walked over to Watson and stood before him, feet wide apart.

Watson sneered at him. "Why, any fool knows a barkin' dog tells Indians where we're campin'."

"Just who are you callin' a *fool?*" Jason's father pushed his hat back on his head and stepped closer.

Watson turned to the others, his puffy face flushing. "You men want to be scalped some night in your beds, do you?" There was a murmur from the crowd.

"All right, then. I say, shoot the critter an' be done with it." He patted the leather holster at his side. "Just you give me the word an' I'll take care of him myself."

Jason gasped. He clutched Scout tighter.

"*I'm* giving you the word, Watson!" Pa was yelling now, shaking his fist. "You lay one finger on my boy's dog an' you'll be mighty sorry. You'll answer to *me!*"

Jason could hardly believe it! Pa was actually taking Scout's side!

Watson moved back, his hand still resting on his holster. "You don't scare me none, Bartow. You're a bag of wind . . . a blowhard . . ."

"Eat them words!" Pa grabbed Watson by the neck of his shirt and pulled him so close that their noses nearly touched. "Take that back, or else . . ."

Watson jerked at his holster. "Look out, Pa! He's got a gun!" Jason shouted, running out of the shadows. He couldn't keep still and let Pa get shot like that bullwacker!

Pa whirled around, surprised to see him, looking away from Watson for a fraction of a second. In that second Wat-

40

son's fist swung up and hit Pa's eye with a sickening *sock*! Pa staggered, then sent a quick right to Watson's jaw, knocking him to the ground.

"Hit him again, Pa!"

Watson was struggling to his feet. Just then Scout grabbed the leg of his pants, growling and yanking for all he was worth. McDermott pulled the dog off. He stepped between Pa and Watson, separating them with his big, outstretched arms. "What in tarnation d'you think you're doin'? Didn't I jest get done sayin' we'd have no more hassles? Was I wastin' my breath tryin' to talk some sense into you greenhorns?" He shook both of them a little, then let them go.

Watson's nose was bleeding. He wiped it with the back of his hand. Pa was touching his eye as if it hurt some.

McDermott reached for Watson's gun. "Best let me keep that, same as I'm keepin' the one belongs to Morgan here. Leastwise, till you cool off some."

"But the dog . . ." Watson sputtered.

"Forgit the dog. He ain't done no real harm. Nor likely to, neither." McDermott looked over at Scout, sitting there on his haunches, head cocked to one side, listening. "Leave him be." McDermott turned to the men, who were crowded around. "Anybody got anythin' more to say? No? Wal then, this meetin's over an' done." And he walked away.

Watson left, too, muttering to himself. The crowd broke up.

On the way back to the wagon, Pa was silent. Jason wanted to thank him for the way he'd defended Scout. He wanted to tell him he was glad he'd beaten Watson. But he couldn't. Pa still looked too grim.

"Henry! You've been fighting!" Ma touched Pa's cheek. It was swelling fast. "You and Watson again! How did it start?"

She listened as Pa told her the story. He winced when she

pressed a cold, wet cloth against his eye. "That'll be black and blue in the morning," she said. She glanced at Jason. "Well, I'm glad your Pa stood up for your dog, anyway."

"I don't know why I did," Pa grumbled. "He's not worth it. I said once before an' I'll say it again, 'trouble' is his middle name. He's sure brought *us* enough." He held his hand to his head, as if it ached. "But he won't bring us any more—after Laramie."

Jason's heart was suddenly a heavy rock in his chest, weighing him down with sadness. Pa hadn't changed a bit, then. That fight with Watson was just to save his own pride in front of the men. Now he was more bound than ever to be rid of the dog.

8

The next day they came to the Platte river, as McDermott said they would. It didn't look like much, Jason thought. It was hard to believe they needed to be afraid of it. Gray-brown and sluggish, it wound across the land like a giant snake. There were just a few trees on its banks, some dusty-looking willows.

The wagons halted. Everyone got out and waited for McDermott to tell them what to do. Jason stood beside his family's wagon, his fingers tracing the notches he'd made in its wood. Twenty of them. They were halfway to Fort Laramie now.

"You comin', Bartow?" McDermott called to Jason's father. He hadn't forgotten Pa's offer to help. "We'd best get goin'. Almost midday." He squinted up at clouds that hid the sun.

Pa threw a saddle on Harry. Harry was gray-brown, too, like the Platte. He followed McDermott's horse slowly into the water.

The two horses took a zigzag path as they went along, stopping often to make sure of solid footing.

Pa and McDermott had cut willow branches and now they stuck them into the riverbed. There was no strong current to the river, so the willow sticks held firm. The tops of them showed on each side of the path the horses were taking, marking the right way so plain that nobody could mistake it.

The Platte was shallow, all right. It came just up to the flanks of the horses. Even so, they acted afraid and had to be urged along. Jason figured they knew, even better than anybody, how tricky that riverbed was.

Once Harry floundered in it, stumbling. The muddy water came up past his chest. He struggled to get his balance, almost throwing Pa. Jason strained to see. He looked over at Ma, wondering how she was taking it. She had her eyes shut and her hands clasped together, and he knew she was saying a prayer that Pa would be safe.

Pa yelled and McDermott wheeled around to help him. He grabbed Harry by the bridle and gave a hard yank. With a toss of his mane, Pa's horse steadied himself. Then they went on.

Jason whistled softly. That was a close one! Would it be like that all the way? Maybe worse?

He watched, not moving a muscle, until the two men had crossed the river and come back. Then he ran to meet them, ahead of Ma and Abbie. Scout, glad to see Harry again, nipped at the horse's hooves, almost getting himself trampled by them.

"You kin go over now," McDermott told everyone. "Single file, mind. An' make mighty certain you stay in the bounds of them markers."

"Let me ride Harry this time, Pa," Jason begged.

"I dunno about that." His father looked doubtful. "This danged river has him skittish. Mebbe you can't handle him."

"I *can*, Pa. He'll do what I say. Honest, he will!" He smoothed the gelding's soft muzzle. "And you've got the oxen. Ma can't drive 'em alone."

"Mebbe you're right." Pa glanced at the team, yoked and ready. "They can be stubborn as all get out, an' your Ma's too tenderhearted to put the whip to 'em like she should." He hesitated. " 'Course, McDermott would probably be willin' to take on another horse besides his own . . ."

But Jason was bound he'd do it. He didn't want to ride over in the wagon with Abbie and Ma. "You don't need McDermott, Pa," he insisted. "Not when you've got me. I'm past eleven now, don't forget."

Pa laughed. "Almost a man, are you? I reckon I'll have to let you prove it, then." He held Harry while Jason mounted. "Keep a tight rein, now. That horse has a mind of his own. Don't let him get the notion he can go wherever he has a hankerin' to."

"I won't, Pa."

Jason sat tall in the saddle, his back straight as a rod, yet easy, so that Harry would know he wasn't edgy at all.

Abbie poked her head, in its checked sunbonnet, around the edge of the wagon. "I'll keep Scout here in the front seat with me," she called back.

"Well, see that you hold onto him," Jason told her.

They started into the river. Harry reared and snorted, whinnying, not wanting to go at first. But Jason gripped the reins firmly and dug his heels into the gelding's flanks, to show him who was boss.

As the water rose higher, surging against his legs, Jason took a deep breath. This was more like it. This was *real* adventure! He took another deep breath. He could smell Harry's sweating flesh—a good, strong horse smell that he liked. He could smell the river, too. It was kind of foul and reminded him of an old barrel they'd kept at home to catch rain. The slats of the barrel had been covered with greenish mold. The Platte didn't look moldy like the barrel—not on top, anyway. It was hard to tell what the bottom was like, what with the slime and quicksand . . .

He'd best not think about that, though. He put his mind on Harry, keeping him on the winding path the willow sticks marked out. He couldn't help tensing some, staring straight ahead at the canvas of their wagon. Could Pa make the oxen mind? Or would they take off, plunging out of bounds? If they did that, heavy as they were, they'd be sure to trap the wagon in the mire. He could hear his father shout and slap them smartly with the whip. The wheels moved through the water with a churning sound, creaking as they turned. Now and then Pa glanced behind, to make sure Jason was coming.

They weren't far now from the opposite shore. Jason flicked at Harry with his heels, hurrying him a little. Then he pulled back hard on the reins. Whoa! Pa's oxen, just ahead, had halted all of a sudden. They'd thrown the wagon off balance so it was swaying and lurching from side to side like crazy! It tipped, and something slid off into the water. Scout!

Pa yelled, cracking the whip against the oxen's hides. The wagon righted again and went on.

But where was Scout? Jason leaned over Harry's neck, searching for him. There he was! He was paddling for all he was worth, his head bobbing up and down like a cork, trying to get to the wagon.

Scout was swimming hard, and could probably make it to shore on his own, close as it was now. But Jason didn't want to take that chance. He slapped Harry with the reins, urging him ahead. When they reached Scout, Jason scooped the dog up and held him safely against the horn of the saddle.

But then Jason looked around with a start. They had gone past the willow markers! He'd been so anxious to get Scout that he'd forgotten all about them!

Quickly, he tried to wheel Harry back where he belonged, but Harry balked. Jason dug his heels into the horse's flanks. Still Harry didn't go ahead. He was *trying* to—Jason could tell that plain enough. Every muscle quivered as he strained. His forelegs thrashed, but something held his hind ones fast. Jason went cold with fear. This was quicksand, for sure. He tried to call for help but he couldn't make a sound. All he could do was cling to the saddle—and to Scout.

Then, with a sudden lunge, Harry broke free! The mire made a loud sucking sound as the horse scrambled from it. Harry walked slowly on.

They reached shore right after Pa and the wagon did. Scout quickly leaped from the saddle, but Jason wasn't in any hurry. Pa was watching him. It seemed as if his eyes would bore a hole right through him.

"Don't ever ask to ride Harry again," Pa said.

"But, why?"

"Because you haven't got good sense, that's why. I saw what you did! Risking your neck—and the fine horse I trusted you with—all for that mutt!" He gave Scout a look of disgust. "I'm warnin' you, son! I've had about all I can take." He shook his finger at Jason. "If that dog does *one* more thing to bring trouble down on us we're leavin' him behind—no matter where we are!"

Jason turned to his mother, but she just nodded her head and said, "Your Pa's right. It's hard enough for us, just getting ourselves to Oregon without the worry of . . ." She wiped her eyes on the corner of her apron. "Oh, Jason! When I think of what might have happened to you back there, all on account of *him*!"

Scout was whimpering, beating his tail on the ground. He knows what they're saying about him, Jason thought. He knows Ma doesn't want him now, either.

Ma had begun to like the dog. Jason had half hoped she'd take his side when they got to Fort Laramie, talk to Pa, maybe get him to soften. Now he couldn't count on her anymore.

He picked Scout up and walked away sadly. "You've just got me," he told him. "Nobody else."

9

Two weeks went by. Jason cut more notches in the wagon, sorry when each one was finished. It meant little time was left for him and Scout—unless he could think of what to do. Sometimes he lay awake, curled up with the dog in his blanket, trying hard to come up with an idea. Once or twice he about decided they'd run away, the two of them. But then he realized how foolish that notion was. It would bring grief to Ma and Pa, too. He didn't want that.

Sunday came again, which meant the train would stop for the day. Most of the folks thought it was wrong to travel on the Sabbath. McDermott didn't, though. He was all for pushing ahead fast as they could, Sunday or no Sunday.

"We're runnin' behind as it is," he kept reminding them. But he always gave in, in spite of his grumbling. "Don't forgit," he'd say, "we still got them Rockies to cross after Fort Laramie. An' I don't aim to be snowbound for the winter."

Winter, McDermott told them many times, might be as early as October in the Rockies, and to be trapped there would mean certain death. Jason had listened, open-mouthed, as

49

the mountain man told them about the Donner Party—folks going west like them who had been caught by a blizzard in the mountains. It had happened just three years ago, in 1847. Most of the party had died of starvation. They had eaten the bark of trees trying to stay alive. Some had boiled their harnesses and boots and tried to chew the softened leather. McDermott hinted they'd been driven to do even worse things. It made Jason shudder to think of it. He sure didn't want that to happen to *them*.

On Sundays there was always a prayer meeting. Since no preacher had joined their train, there was nobody to give a sermon. But they made do with singing hymns, and Jason's father read a verse or two from the Bible they'd brought along. Then everybody bowed their heads in silence, giving thanks to the Lord for taking care of them as He had.

A few men didn't come to the prayer meeting. They were mostly the bullwackers, a rough bunch hired to drive oxen for folks who couldn't manage by themselves. They played cards or went hunting instead.

McDermott usually showed up, though, taking off his broad-rimmed hat and twirling it in his hands as if he wasn't exactly sure what to do with it. Sundays were about the only time Jason saw the mountain man without his hat. It was all he could do to keep from staring. He wondered if McDermott's legs got as cramped as his did, sitting there on the ground with them folded under him, Indian fashion.

This particular Sunday the service seemed to go on and on. Pa had picked an extra long piece of Scripture to read— all about Moses and the Israelites in the wilderness. Jason smothered a yawn. He looked over at Abbie, asleep on Ma's lap. Scout was dozing, too, his little black nose tucked between his paws. The dog roused, though, when Pa stopped reading and Watson, in his whiny voice, said, "Can I have a word?"

Pa scowled at Watson, but that didn't stop him. "I got to thinkin', folks," Watson said, "how we're just like them Israelites. How we've been spared and showed the way."

"Uh-oh," Jason said to himself. They were sure to be there a lot longer when Watson sounded off like that, so pious and mealymouthed. He'd done it before.

"Amen to that, Brother Watson," somebody said, trying to cut him short. It didn't work, though. Watson went right on, droning away like a bee in clover. He started quoting some Scripture on his own—the part about the Israelites making themselves a golden calf to worship. Jason sat up straight, all ears. Watson was looking right at Pa. "Now that reminds me of a young cow I had," he started. Pa's face flushed. He was gripping the Bible so hard his knuckles turned white.

McDermott jumped to his feet. "I smell somethin' burnin'," he said, sniffing. "Ladies? Did one of you leave dinner too long on the fire?"

"Oh, mercy!" Ma said, hurrying off, taking Abbie with her. The other women left, too. That ended the service, for *that* day, anyway.

Jason was glad nothing had happened to spoil Sunday dinner. It was the best meal of the week. Earlier that morning Pa had shot a couple of prairie hens. Ma roasted them and fixed some cornbread. She used the last of the dried apples they'd brought to make a pie. "There won't be another for a good while so make the most of it," she told them.

After dinner, when the chores were done, everyone rested in the shade of the wagons. "This day's a scorcher," Pa said.

"It *is* close," Ma agreed. She fanned herself with her sunbonnet. "I can hardly get my breath. I wonder if it might be going to rain?"

"Sure is, ma'am." McDermott, who had joined them, looked up at the sky. There wasn't a cloud in it, and Jason wondered if he could see something they couldn't. "Yessir. I wouldn't be a'tall surprised if we was to have a real storm. They come up mighty quick out here on the plains. Do a sight of damage, too."

He turned to Jason's father. "First clap of thunder you hear you know what to do, Bartow. Get your livestock rounded up. Drive some stakes an' anchor down that wagon. It wouldn't hurt none, either, to throw some of them chains around the wheels, fasten 'em together."

Jason listened carefully, in case he was asked to help. McDermott must be expecting a storm worse than any they had back in Pennsylvania. He was already hurrying off to tell the others. He called over his shoulder, "That widow, Mrs. Kelley, could probably stand some helpin'. I'll see she gets it." Jason remembered how Mrs. Kelley's husband had been killed, just a few days ago, in an accident. An ornery horse he'd been trying to shoe had kicked him in the head and he'd died within an hour.

"Come on, son. Give me a hand," Pa said.

Jason and Pa had just finished with what they had to do when a jagged streak of lightning suddenly lit up the sky. It reminded Jason of fireworks he'd seen at the county fair one Fourth of July. The boom of thunder that followed was so loud it had all the horses whinnying, rearing up on their hind legs, and yanking at the ropes that tethered them. The cattle and oxen began to bellow.

"Here she comes!" Pa pointed to black clouds now spreading from the horizon clear across the sky. "Get into the wagon, all of you!"

Jason boosted Ma and Abbie up into the wagon, then turned. "How about you, Pa? Aren't you coming?"

Pa shook his head. "You go on. Get inside, like I said. Maybe Mac needs me. If them cattle break loose they'll stampede for sure."

Jason took a last look around. Everyone was scurrying to the wagons for cover. Women were snatching up their children and running. Men were yelling. It was turning dark as night. Cold, too. He pulled up the collar of his shirt. A strong wind had started to blow, sweeping everything that was loose and in its path ahead of it. Big clumps of dry grass, like balls in a game giants might be playing, rolled by. The prairie tossed like an angry sea. A spatter of hail hit the ground, bouncing up from it, and the livestock moaned, half crazy with fear.

Then Jason remembered Scout. Where was he? Jason had been too busy to notice he was gone. Now he called and whistled, but the dog didn't come, which wasn't like him at all.

Maybe he was hiding under the wagon, too scared to come out. Jason crawled between the wheels to check. He wasn't there.

Maybe he was inside? The wagon flaps were tied shut, but he pushed against the canvas, calling to Ma, "Where's Scout?"

"I don't know. Isn't he with you?" Ma reached out, trying to hold him back. "Get in here! It's going to pour any minute now. Don't go off looking for that dog!"

"I *got* to, Ma!" Jason pulled away from her. "I got to find him!"

He scrambled under all the other wagons, calling Scout, shouting until his voice was lost in the wailing of the wind. It was blowing harder now. Jason braced himself, facing into each new gust that tore at him. He dodged a dead branch of a tree that came flying through the air. The storm was cutting through a cluster of cottonwoods. He stumbled on.

Lightning pierced the sky again. Now a flood of rain came, pelting Jason. He could feel its sharp sting, like a million needles, against his face. His soaked clothes clung to his skin; the wind whipped his pants around his legs. He brushed his dripping hair from his eyes. He could hardly see, but it was plain there was nobody else out in this, unless Pa was hunting for *him*.

He had one more place to look, then he'd have to give up and run for the wagon. He hadn't searched the corral yet, where the livestock were herded together. McDermott and the other men had thrown up a hasty barricade for them. Now he fought his way there.

He found Harry first. The horse came to him, close as his tether would let him. Jason reached for his muzzle. Then he heard a pitiful howl!

"Scout! Where are you?" He groped past Harry in the darkness, wind and rain lashing at him.

The next blaze of lightning revealed the dog, huddled against the side of the corral. When he saw Jason he howled again, but he didn't come running. What was wrong?

Jason rushed to him. He knelt down and gathered him close. Why, there was a cord around Scout's neck! He'd been tied! Tethered to a stake, like Harry and the rest of the horses. No wonder he didn't come.

Jason fumbled at the cord, trying to undo it with wet,

54

slippery fingers. Scout made it even harder, leaping at him, flailing with his paws.

Who could have done this, Jason asked himself? The more he struggled to free Scout the madder he got. *Who* could have done it? Not Pa. No matter what he thought of the dog he'd never be *that* mean. Not McDermott, either, nor any of the men, unless it was Watson . . .

Another flash of lightning and Jason was able to see well enough to untie the knot. Scout pulled loose and started racing in circles, he was that glad to be free.

But what was that shiny thing on the ground, close to the stake where the dog had been tied? Jason picked it up and turned it over in his fingers. It was a pocketknife, bigger than the one he had, the blade half open. Luke had a knife like that. He'd showed it to Jason once, bragging that it had cost all of fifty cents, back in Independence. Luke had cut his initials into its wood handle. Jason felt for them now, tracing the crooked *L* and *W*. He snapped the blade shut and put the knife in his pocket. It was Luke's, all right! This was Luke's doing! No doubt about it.

With Scout at his heels, he ran back to the wagon, wet and shivering, shaking with anger. Ma held open the canvas flap. She took Scout when Jason handed the dog up to her. Jason climbed inside.

Ma held a quilt out to him. "Here, wrap up in this. Get out of those soaked clothes before you catch your death!" She got a rag and rubbed Scout dry, too.

When Pa came, a few minutes later, Jason thought for sure he'd be in for a scolding. But Pa just glanced at him and nodded, his face grim, then took Abbie in his arms and tried to comfort her. Abbie was crying, afraid of the storm.

The wind was howling, making the wagon creak and groan, tossing it from side to side. It seemed as though it would push them right over. Rain was coming through in some places where the canvas was worn thin. Jason crawled back and lay down on Ma's bed, the quilt around him. The bed was damp and musty, and smelled of wet feathers. But he didn't mind. He was just glad to be there with Scout curled up against him.

He was so cold now, trembling all over. Even his teeth were clicking together and he couldn't stop them. He shut his eyes. It felt as though the wagon was going round and round. He knew that couldn't be so, but just the same, he went round with it. Faster and faster. Then he was falling, down, down, with nothing to hold on to, except Scout's furry head.

For six days and nights Jason lay on Ma's feather bed, tossing and turning. He was so sick that he didn't even notice when the storm stopped and their wagon moved on.

First he was racked by chills. He could hear Scout whimper, but he sounded far away. He could hear Ma talking to him, but what she said didn't seem to make any sense. He only knew that, from time to time, she brought stones, hot from the campfire and wrapped in cloth, and put them close to his feet. She filled a sock with ashes and held it against his sore throat. He felt warm for a little while and was able to fall asleep.

But then he woke up, burning with fever. Dripping with sweat, he tried to throw off the quilt that covered him. His head ached as though a dozen hammers were beating on it. Even the wet cloths Ma put on it didn't help. She tried to get him to drink some tea she'd brewed from wild cherry bark. He couldn't swallow it, though. It stuck in his throat.

Once or twice he felt Pa's hand on his forehead, not heavy like it usually was, but light and easy. "Will he be all right?" Pa kept asking.

He also heard Pa say, "How about the dog? Shouldn't we keep him outside, away from the boy?" Jason roused at that and groped for Scout.

"Leave him be, Henry," Ma said quickly. "The boy needs him. Can't you see that?"

Nights were worst of all. When Jason finally went to sleep, he had awful nightmares about Indians with knives, ready to scalp him, or a man who looked like Watson, only bigger, shooting at him with a rifle. He would wake up screaming. Ma would say softly, "There, there. It was just a bad dream." He couldn't be sure, though, until he touched Scout's fur. And Scout was always there.

On the morning of the seventh day, Jason woke to feel the dog's cold nose against his cheek. He was better, he could tell. He was still weak and ached all over, but he was able to lift his head. Scout whined in a happy kind of way. Jason patted him, then lay back again.

The first rays of sun were making a dappled pattern on top of the wagon. Jason stared at it awhile, listening to folks talking outside. A horse snorted, then sneezed and whinnied. Pans and skillets clattered. Breakfast was cooking. He could smell the bacon frying. He raised himself up on his elbows. Why, he was hungry! For the first time since he took sick he wanted to eat!

Pa stuck his head inside the wagon and when Jason told him he grinned. "I reckon you're cured, son!" he exclaimed, and went out to give Ma the good news.

"The Lord be praised!" Jason heard her cry.

When she brought his food, McDermott was right behind her. He seemed to fill the whole wagon. Bending over the bed, he looked bigger than ever to Jason. "Glad to hear you've licked the fever, boy," he said. He took off his hat. Jason looked right into his eyes, under their grizzled brows. "Now don't you go gettin' frisky too soon. Take it slow. You hear?"

After he had gone, Jason asked Ma, "What day is it, anyway? Are we almost to Fort Laramie?" He was afraid to hear her answer.

"Not quite." She plumped a pillow behind him and rested his shoulders against it. "Mr. McDermott says we're a little behind schedule. We've got three more good days of travel ahead of us, he says."

"Has Pa"—Jason swallowed the spoonful of porridge she gave him, then went on—"Has Pa changed his mind? About me keepin' Scout, I mean?"

She smoothed his hair for a minute before she said, "Now don't you go worrying about such things. Here. Eat every bite of this. It'll help you get well and strong."

"But what did Pa say?" Jason pushed away the food. "I *got* to know."

"Why, nothing. He hasn't had a thought for anything but you, Jason. Neither of us has. You gave us such a scare." Her eyes got all misty.

"Well, find out for me, Ma. Will you?" He reached for her hand. "Ask him. He'll tell *you*."

"All right," she promised and left, patting his pillow one more time.

He closed his eyes. His head was pounding again. Three days, that was all. Three days. Three days. Pa had been sorry when he was sick. Maybe he'd been sorry enough to change his mind. Maybe . . .

That evening after supper Jason listened to his parents talking. They were sitting just outside the wagon. Pa was saying the axle of the wagon needed some grease to stop its screeching. Ma mentioned they were almost out of flour.

"We'll get more at Fort Laramie," Pa said.

"Oh, yes. Fort Laramie . . ." Ma hesitated. "Which reminds me. Jason was asking today about the dog."

"What about the dog?"

Jason listened harder.

"Well, Jason was wondering . . . what's to become of him, once we reach the fort. He's hoping maybe you—"

"I thought that was settled." Pa sounded brisk and matter-of-fact. "Like I told him, we'll give the dog to some family stationed there. I'll ask the sergeant to find him a good home."

Jason clenched his hands until the nails dug into his flesh. He might have known Pa wouldn't change his mind.

There was a silence outside.

"Now what's the matter?" his father asked gruffly. "Somethin' I said don't set right with you, Mary. I can always tell. You get that sorry look."

"I'm sorry for *you*, Henry Bartow." Ma's voice wavered, then got stronger. "How you can sit there and say such a hard thing is beyond me! Why, you ought to be down on your knees right this minute, thanking Providence for sparing your son. But instead you're . . . you're figuring how to rid him of the one creature he really loves!"

Although Jason couldn't see her, he knew her eyes—blue like Abbie's—were flashing with anger.

"Hold on! You needn't get yourself all riled up just because—"

"Have you thought what it'll mean to the boy? Losing that dog?"

"I reckon he'll get over it soon enough." Pa sounded edgy, as if he knew he had to stand up to Ma. "Besides, he knew this was comin'. I gave him fair warning, right from the start. I can understand him wantin' to have a dog and mebbe one of these days, when we get us our farm in Oregon, he can. But the sooner he finds out he can't get everything he has a hankerin' for the better off he'll be. Life's not easy for *any* of us, y'know."

"Oh, you're heartless, you are!" Jason wasn't sure, but he thought his mother was beginning to cry. "When I think how faithful Scout's been . . . Why, he stayed right by Jason the whole time he was sick. Remember? Wouldn't touch a bit of food. Just lay there, watching the boy."

"The trouble with you, Mary, is you're too soft." Pa was moving about now. Jason could hear his boots scrape the ground. "An' you're forgetting one thing, aren't you? Whose fault was it the boy came down with the fever? Answer me that! If he hadn't been out in that storm looking for the dog, if he hadn't gotten soaked to the skin . . ."

Jason heard his father walk away. The argument was over. Pa had won. He always did.

11

When they were ready to pull out next morning, Pa asked, "How about it, son? D'you feel well enough to ride up front with me?"

"Yes, sir." Jason straddled the seat of the wagon. He settled himself, and Scout jumped up on his lap like he always did. We won't have many more rides together, Jason thought, fighting back a wave of sadness. It helped some when he took a deep breath, filling his lungs with the fresh air of the plains.

Ma hadn't said anything to him about last night. He hadn't said anything to her, either. He didn't have to.

"We'll be in Laramie in about three days." Pa was looking at him from the corner of his eye. Jason figured Pa expected him to ask again about the dog. He didn't, though. It wouldn't do any good.

He sat there, not saying a word, watching the heads of the oxen bob up and down, listening to the creak of the wheels. Every turn of them was bringing him and Scout closer to the time when they would have to part. I'm not gonna give him up! I won't! he kept telling himself. But he knew in his heart there was nothing else he *could* do.

He rubbed Scout's ears, trying to imagine what it would be like, handing him over to some other boy at the fort. The dog peered up into his face. Did Scout understand?

"You're mighty quiet settin' there, Jason." Pa broke the silence after they had gone a mile or two. "Sure you aren't ailin' again?"

"No, sir," Jason said. He glanced back at the wagons behind them. Pa's wagon was first today. McDermott saw to it that they took turns. That was the only fair way. Then nobody had to be last in line for long, taking more than their share of dust.

The land was still flat as a johnnycake, stretching ahead to the blue horizon. But they were coming into buffalo country now. There weren't many trees and McDermott said they'd have to use buffalo chips for fuel when they made their camp fire. Jason didn't much like the idea of having to gather up those dried pieces of dung, but he bet he'd have to do it as part of his chores.

McDermott was riding just ahead. He took off his hat and waved it, pointing to a herd of buffalo, which were thundering along in the distance. They were gone almost as soon as Jason spied them, disappearing like a black cloud against the sky.

"If they'd been a mite closer we'd have had ourselves fresh meat for supper," Pa said. He patted the rifle at his side. Once before, they'd met up with some buffalo. McDermott had led the men in a hunt. Pa had shot a fat one, so Jason knew how good the steaks tasted, roasted over the fire. Some of the meat had been dried over a slow flame and then cut into strips that McDermott called "jerky." They were tough to chew, but they would sure come in handy if your stomach was empty.

Now and then, as they rode along, Jason saw a high mound

63

of rock rise from the level plain. They must be getting closer to the mountains, he decided. These were just a sample of what was ahead. Once they passed Fort Laramie, McDermott told them, the Rockies would begin. Then it would be *real* hard going.

They stopped for nooning in front of one of the big mounds, because it offered a little shade. "This here's Scott's Bluff," McDermott said, pointing to its steep sides. "Indians call it 'the hill too hard to go around,' but I reckon it won't keep *us* back none. I know the way when we're ready to move on.

"There's water yonder behind them cottonwoods," he said. Jason was glad to see a few trees. Maybe when they stopped tonight there would be some, too. He might not have to pick up buffalo chips after all.

He got down from the wagon slowly. He sure was tired. He didn't want Pa to notice, though, so he hustled over to help unhitch the team.

"No need for you to do that," Pa told him. "You look kind of peaked. Better rest awhile."

Jason leaned against one of the trees, watching folks water their livestock, listening to the lap of tongues as the animals drank at the little stream. Today Scout didn't seem a bit interested in the cattle and horses, which wasn't like him. He just lay there, quiet and still, with his head on Jason's knee. He sat up, though, with a start when Luke came along.

Luke was leading his father's cows to the water, whistling a tune to himself. He saw Jason and stopped short. His face got a shamed look.

"Hullo," he said gruffly. He turned, as though he wanted to leave, but he couldn't—not with the cattle pressing against him.

64

Scout growled low in his throat.

"I heard you was sick," Luke said.

Jason just nodded. He fingered Luke's knife in his pocket. He'd been carrying it, meaning to show it to him first chance he got. He could feel the rounded corners of it, and the grooves in the wood that spelled *LW*. Yessir. He'd show it to him. He meant to tell him a thing or two when he did. All that had gone through his head, over and over, when he tossed on Ma's feather bed, when he was burning with fever and with something even worse—hate that was festering inside him. He'd pictured to himself the showdown he'd have with Luke, once he was up and about and a whole lot stronger. He'd tell him just what he thought of anybody who'd pull such a low trick on a dog. Then he'd punch Luke hard, smack in the nose, make him say he was sorry . . .

"I sure am sorry."

Jason sat up straight. What was Luke saying? Did he hear him right?

"Yeah, I'm real sorry you got the fever," Luke mumbled, head down, digging the toe of his boot into the ground.

Jason reached in his pocket, pulled out the knife, and handed it to him. "Why, that's mine!" Luke exclaimed. He stared at it and then at Jason. "Where'd you find it?"

"In the corral. Next to that stake Scout was tied to." Jason looked him right in the eye.

Luke flushed. "Well, I never meant no real harm . . ." He swallowed a couple of times. "I never figgered you'd stay out in that storm like you did."

Scout stopped growling. He thumped his tail a couple of times. Jason put his arm around the dog.

Luke was just standing there, looking miserable, waiting . . .

All of a sudden the anger and hate that had been inside Jason melted. He felt almost sorry for Luke.

"Forget it," he said. "*I aim to.*"

As soon as the words were out he felt a whole lot better. Light and easy. He was glad he said it. Somehow, being mad at a person made you feel mean. The longer you stayed mad the worse it got, until you didn't even like *yourself* much. But making up with somebody, after they admitted they'd done you wrong—well, that was sure a good feeling.

Luke's face brightened. "Say, Jason. Tell you what. Tonight after supper, when the chores are done, let's you an' me go huntin' for arrowheads! The Indians—"

Ma came running over just then. "Have you seen Abbie?" she cried. She was breathing hard, like she did when she was upset about something.

"Why no, Ma." Jason said, standing up. "Isn't she playing with the other little kids?"

"No. I went to call her to come and eat. The children were having a game of hide-and-seek, but they said she hadn't been with them for quite awhile." Ma twisted her hands in her apron. "One little girl told me Abbie said she was going to get a hiding place where *nobody'd* find her! Oh, Jason!" She clutched his arm. "Do you reckon she's wandered off and can't find her way back? Do you reckon she's—"

"Now don't you worry, Ma." Jason tried to sound as if everything was all right. "She can't be far away. I'll go fetch her."

"I'll help you look for her," Luke volunteered. "Soon's I tend to these cows."

Ma was staring up at the steep sides of Scott's Bluff. "Mercy! I hope she didn't try to climb—"

"Now Mrs. Bartow, don't go thinkin' the worst," Luke broke in. "She's likely still hidin' out somewhere. We'll find her."

"That's right, Ma." Jason put his arm around his mother's waist. "Quit frettin'. Why, we'll be back with her before you can say Abigail Genevieve Bartow!"

12

It wasn't that easy, though. Jason, with Scout bounding along beside him, looked everywhere. He asked all the grown-ups and children if they'd seen Abbie. Nobody had. Soon Luke came to help like he said he would.

"We'll have to get Pa," Jason said at last. "He'll know what to do."

Back at the wagon Pa was talking to McDermott about Abbie. They'd been searching for her, too. Everyone was crowded around, asking questions. "Who? The Bartow girl? Missing, you say? How long?"

Ma was crying and some of the women were trying to comfort her. "I know how *I'd* feel if it was my little Cora who was lost," Mrs. Kelley was saying. She had her new baby in her arms.

"You don't reckon . . ." Pa pointed to the Bluff. "She wouldn't have tried to climb up there, would she?"

"Not likely." McDermott shook his head. "Not that little tyke, with them short legs she's got."

Jason started to tell them Abbie was used to the mountains they had back in Pennsylvania. They weren't as steep as this, though. But nobody listened. McDermott was calling the men together to form a search party. "Spread out, you fellers! Cover all the ground you kin!"

Ma, her skirts lifted high above her black shoes, came running after Pa and McDermott. "Wait! I'm going with you!"

Everybody scattered in different directions. Jason and Scout set out together, but Scout ran on ahead, his twisted tail wagging furiously. Jason raced after him. Maybe he'd caught Abbie's scent? After all, hadn't McDermott said he had all the makings of a coon hound?

A few minutes later, though, Scout was back, looking sheepish. It had been a false lead.

Jason sighed and went on looking. Scout seemed to want to sniff at every rock. Jason urged him to go faster. He was getting tight with worry himself, now. So many things could have happened to Abbie. He thought of rattlers, slithering through the tall grass. Bears, maybe. And they were still in wolf country. He hadn't seen any, not yet. McDermott said they mostly stayed hidden away from folks. But a few nights ago he'd heard a strange kind of howling that sent shivers down his spine.

After awhile everyone came back to the wagons, tired, hot, and discouraged. Pa and McDermott had even gone up the side of the Bluff for a short piece.

McDermott took off his battered hat and wiped the sweat from his face with his sleeve. "Bartow"—he cleared his throat—"I reckon we've got to move on without you. We can't stay here, settin' an' waitin'. We got to git to Laramie afore the food runs out."

69

Pa's mouth hung open, as though he couldn't believe what he was hearing. "You mean . . . But you *can't* just pull out and leave us!"

"I know it sounds hard." The mountain man kept his eyes down, not looking directly at Pa. "But that's how it is. If it was only me, why, man! I'd stick with you, lookin' for that little gal till kingdom come. I got to think what's best for the whole outfit, though."

"Tell me the truth, Mac." Jason's father lowered his voice. Jason knew it was so Ma wouldn't hear. "You don't think there's any chance for her, do you? You think the Indians—"

"I didn't say that, Bartow." McDermott kicked a stone with his boot and sent it flying. "I'm jest sayin' I got to consider *all* these folks, not jest you." He got busy tightening the cinch of his horse's saddle. "Now we'll head on for Laramie. It'll take us a good two days to git there. We'll go slow. You kin catch up with us once you find your little gal." He cleared his throat again.

Jason wondered, like Pa, if the mountain man had given up on Abbie. He was so smart. Maybe he knew something he wasn't telling?

"Supposin' we *never* find her?" Jason wanted to ask. He didn't, though, on account of Ma. That would make her feel worse.

Now Pa was saying, "I dunno as I *can* follow you, Mac. I could get lost myself in these parts, easy. What if I miss the trail?"

"You ain't goin' to miss it." McDermott shifted the wad of tobacco in his cheek. "All you got to do is keep to the right. Then, once you're past that divide in the Bluff— see it, yonder?—why, you swing left. There's an old, dead

70

cottonwood—leastwise there was last time I come this way. Now when you git to it you want to go left agin . . ."

Pa was shaking his head, puzzled. McDermott muttered something under his breath about "greenhorns." He stooped down and started scratching in the dry earth with a stick. "Look-a-here. I'll make you a map."

Jason and Pa both leaned over his shoulder and watched carefully as he drew it. Jason tried to remember everything he said, just in case Pa might need to know later, but it was hard.

Once the stick McDermott was holding broke and he had to look for another. Then he made a mistake and wiped it all out with his boot, starting over again. Jason decided it was maybe easier for him to do things himself than tell other folks how.

He kept mentioning signs to look for along the way. The wreck of an overturned wagon, lying on its side, rotting. A heap of rocks with a wooden cross on top of them, where somebody had been buried. Jason knew the rocks were there to keep wolves away. He shivered. He couldn't help thinking what might happen to *them* once they were separated from the rest of the train and on their own.

"Got that?" McDermott finished and rocked back on his heels.

"I . . . reckon so." Pa still sounded doubtful.

Jason could think of lots more questions he wanted to ask. What would happen if just Pa, Ma, and him were still here when it got dark? Were Indians watching them right this minute? If they were, and if they saw the rest of the train go off and leave them, what were they likely to do? He'd felt safe enough before, with all the folks around and the guards on duty. But now, when night came and there was only Pa with his gun . . .

71

Folks were climbing into their wagons, getting ready to pull out. Ma started sobbing and Pa, looking anxious himself, put his arm around her.

McDermott swung up on his horse. He doffed his hat respectfully. "Don't take on so, ma'am," he said. "You'll find that little one of yours. Mebbe catch up with us afore sundown."

He gave the order, "Roll out!" and the wagons started. Jason got a terrible lonely feeling all of a sudden. Scout, beside him, howled mournfully when he saw everyone leaving, which made it all the worse. The folks waved good-bye. Mrs. Kelley, Ma's special friend, leaned out of her wagon and called, "I'll pray for you, Mary."

With a sinking feeling, Jason watched the last white wagon top disappear around the side of the Bluff. *Now* what would they do?

Ma was still crying. Jason hugged her. "Don't, Ma," he begged.

"What are we standin' here for?" Pa said briskly. "We've got at least a few more hours of daylight. Let's start huntin' again."

"That's right." Jason said. He felt a new surge of hope. "And I know just where Scout an' me are bound—up that Bluff." After all, it was the one place nobody had searched very hard, the one place where Abbie might be.

"Oh, be careful!" Ma clung to his arm. "If you were to fall . . . If I lost you, too . . ."

"Let the boy go, Mary," Pa told her. "Let him try."

Jason whistled for Scout, and they trudged off together.

13

They made straight for the Bluff, breaking into a run as they went up its slope. Scout scrambled up the steep side of the mound, scattering a shower of loose stones, looking back to be sure Jason was coming. He's surefooted as a goat, Jason thought, which was more than he could say for himself. He had to figure out which rocks to grab and where to wedge his boots, with their slick leather soles. It slowed him down.

The afternoon sun was hot now on his head and shoulders, and his shirt was soaked with sweat. He stopped to wipe his eyes, shutting them for a second against the glare. "Abbie! Abbie! Where are you?" he yelled again and again, until his throat was dry as prairie dust and his voice cracked. The only answer was his own echo.

Taking a deep breath, he searched the plain below. Maybe up here, high as he was, he'd catch sight of Abbie's pink dress. The land spread out for miles, desolate and barren; there was no sign of any living thing. He got that lonely feeling again. Their wagon looked so tiny, standing by itself. Was Abbie out there? If she was, he couldn't see her.

One thing was sure. She wasn't up on the Bluff. She could never have climbed this far, little as she was. Why, even Scout was ready to call it quits. He had turned around and was coming back, slipping and sliding.

Jason steadied himself with one hand and reached out to help. But Scout went right past him. He had his nose down, sniffing, going in a crazy zigzag kind of way. Jason turned around and went after him, boots scraping as he braked.

They had almost reached level ground when Scout stopped suddenly. Between two big rocks was a crevice, too wide to jump across. Scout was standing there now, peering down into it. His tail began to wag. He let out one shrill yelp, then another.

Jason hurried to the crevice, heart pounding. He looked down. At first he couldn't see anything, it was so dark in there. But Scout kept barking. Jason gripped one of the rocks and leaned over farther. He squinted and looked again. Abbie! It was Abbie!

She was lying all in a heap, limp as her rag doll. The way the rocks hid her, it was no wonder Pa and McDermott had gone right past. He'd never have found her, either, if it hadn't been for Scout!

Scout wasn't barking now. He was whining instead—that mournful whine of his that meant something was wrong. Jason's skin prickled with goose bumps. Abbie was awful still. Her eyes were shut. She wasn't making a sound. Jason swallowed hard. Could she be . . . Was she . . . *dead*?

Scout was clawing at the edge of the rock, trying to get to her. Jason tried, too. He planted his feet and bent over, stretching his arms as far as he could. For a second he had his fingers on Abbie's pinafore. He could feel the soft calico, but then it slipped from him. He had to get a grip on it somehow!

74

He lay down on his belly and wriggled close to the crevice. Then he reached down again. This time he was able to grab her pinafore with both hands. He pulled at it. "Abbie! It's me!"

She gave a little jerk. Her face twitched. Then she opened her eyes. Jason could tell she'd been crying hard, they were so swollen. And when she saw him she started to cry again.

"There now, Abbie." He tried to sound comforting like Ma. "You're gonna be all right, once I get you out of that dang hole. How'd you get yourself in such a fix, anyway?"

"I . . . I fell!"

"Well, try to stand up. Give me your hand and mebbe—"

"I can't. I hurt too much!"

This was more than he could handle, he knew that. "I'm going for Pa," he told her. "You just set tight, hear? I won't be more'n a couple minutes."

"Don't go, Jason!" Her eyes were wide and frightened. "Don't leave me."

"I'm going for Pa," he said firmly. "I'll be right back." He pointed a finger at Scout, who was sitting there, still whining. "Now you stay with her, boy. Mind! You watch out for her."

Jason went down the slope of the Bluff as fast as he dared, clutching at the sharp edge of rocks, his boots skidding. When he got to the bottom, he started yelling. "Pa! Ma! Come quick! I found her!"

They ran to him. "She's down in a big hole!" He gasped for breath. "I tried to get her out but I couldn't."

They all hurried to where Abbie was. Scout was still crouched in the same spot, guarding her. Pa leaned far down. His long arms caught her and pulled her up slowly.

"Oh, my poor baby!" Ma cried. She reached out to take her from his arms. "Henry, is she hurt bad?"

Pa ran his hands over Abbie's small body. "Don't seem to be. No broken bones. Plenty of bruises, though."

He touched a bump on Abbie's forehead and she screamed, "It hurts! It hurts!"

"Of course it does, dear." Ma rocked her, crooning, then gave Pa a worried look. "Do you think she's all right?"

Pa touched her head gently again. He nodded. "She's more scared than anything."

"Didn't you hear me yelling, Abbie?" Jason asked. "I went right past you."

She didn't answer. Her little face had a dazed look.

"That fall must have knocked her out for awhile," Pa said.

Ma snuggled Abbie against her shoulder. "There, there, dear," she said. "It's all over now. You're safe."

"If it wasn't for Scout we might never have found her," Jason said. He swept Scout up and held him over to Abbie. Scout licked her cheek and she smiled.

"We owe a lot to that dog, Henry," Ma said.

"I reckon we do." Pa's fingers tugged at Scout's ear for a minute.

"Then . . . can we keep him . . ." Jason began. But Pa didn't seem to hear. He gathered up Abbie and started down the slope. "Get back to the wagon, fast as you can!" Pa called over his shoulder. "If we leave right away we'll mebbe catch up with the train before nightfall."

"Shouldn't we stay here?" Ma came stumbling after him. "Wait till morning to set out? It'll be dark in about another hour and you said yourself you weren't sure of that trail."

"That was before Mac pointed it out for me, on that map he drew." Pa stopped and turned to her. "Don't you reckon *I* know what's best to do, Mary?" His voice had an edge to it.

76

Jason could tell Pa wasn't all that certain. He didn't want Ma to know, though. "Now hurry up, will you?"

Jason followed after Pa, doing everything he said to do. He fetched more water from the stream to take along. He tied Harry to the back of the wagon. He was helping yoke the oxen when Pa said, real low, "You know, son, there just might be some things Mac told us that slipped my mind." He looked over at Scott's Bluff. The sun had gone behind it now. Shadows on its rocks were turning deep purple. He put his hand on Jason's shoulder. "But mebbe I can count on you to remember."

Could he? Jason wasn't too sure. He said, "Yes, sir." What else *could* he say?

14

"I still think we should have waited till morning," Ma said as they drove away. She kept looking back. "Why, the sun's ready to set. How can you follow those directions Mr. McDermott gave you in the dark? If we can't find the trail . . ."

"I don't want to get lost again!" Abbie cried.

"Nobody's goin' to get lost. Now quit your frettin'," Pa told her. "That goes for you, too, Mary," he said. "Don't you give me credit for having any sense at all? If I'm not sure I'm headed right, I'll stop. We'll spend the night *wherever* we are. That satisfy you?"

Ma was quiet then. Jason could see her lips were thin and tight, the way they got when she was anxious about something. Pa started to hum "Oh! Susanna," but stopped in the middle. He was worried, too, Jason could tell. Only he didn't want the rest of them to know.

Jason didn't feel any too easy himself. He went over and over, in his head, what McDermott had told them. The more he thought about that map the more blurred and mixed-up it was.

He slumped on the seat. He was plenty tired. It had been a hard day. All that hunting for Abbie, and now they were starting out again. He glanced at his father's face, which was pale and strained. He was tired, too.

"Ma, I'm hungry." Abbie was fussing again.

"Hush. We *all* are," Ma said. She passed around some jerky—that dried buffalo meat—and they chewed in silence. They wouldn't stop for supper.

The light was beginning to fade. Shadows, like the long, bony fingers of some ghost, stretched out to them across the land. A knot formed in Jason's stomach. It wasn't because of the jerky, either.

"There! Look yonder!" Pa pointed ahead. "It's the cotton-wood Mac said to watch out for."

"He didn't say there'd be *two* dead trees!" Ma cried.

There were two cottonwoods, all right, both of them de-cayed skeletons. McDermott had mentioned only one. He was never wrong, was he? These were in different places. Which one were they supposed to follow?

"Well, I'll be!" Pa brought the wagon to a quick halt. He took off his hat and scratched his head.

It was Jason who saw the piece of paper fluttering from a limb of the taller tree. "Wait, Pa! Mebbe that's for us. I'll find out."

It was a message from McDermott—only it was written in such a scrawl that neither Jason nor Pa could read it.

"He means for us to turn at this tree, though," Pa said after a minute. "I'm certain of that, anyway."

They went on, fast as the team could go, which wasn't nearly fast enough. They'd never catch up with the rest of the folks before night, Jason thought. They'd have to camp some-where alone, with Indians maybe watching every move they made, waiting to jump them. Like as not, those Indians were following them right now, wanting Harry and the oxen. Maybe wanting some scalps, besides. Jason felt his skin begin to prickle.

"There's the grave Mac told us about," Pa said as their wagon rumbled quickly past the pile of stones with the cross on top. Jason sighed with relief. He was glad they weren't going to spend the night there. The folks who had died— were they trying to get to Laramie, too, he wondered?

Soon Pa halted again. It was nearly dark. He stared ahead, squinting.

"Can't you see, Henry?" Ma asked. "Should I light the lantern?"

"No." Pa held up his hand to stop her. "We'll have to get by without a light." He didn't say why, but Jason figured he didn't want to bring Indians down on them if he could help it.

"I was hoping to keep on till we met up with the folks." Pa ran his sleeve across his eyes. "But I dunno . . ."

"Don't stop, Pa! Please don't!" Jason said. He glanced around at the deepening twilight. Were those shadows moving? "Why, McDermott and the rest might be just around the bend."

Pa climbed down from the wagon. "Come here, son." He motioned for Jason to follow. Scout leaped down, too.

"You see that fork in the trail?"

Jason peered into the dimness. "I . . . I reckon I do." He could hardly make it out.

Pa leaned closer. "For the life of me I can't remember what Mac said about it—whether we ought to go right or left." Pa was whispering now. "Do *you* recollect?"

80

Jason rubbed the palms of his hands against his pants. His throat tightened. Here it was—what he'd been dreading! They were in a tight spot. Pa was counting on him, and he'd have to let him down. He couldn't remember, any more than Pa could. He couldn't guess, either. If he did and was wrong—why, they'd go so far off the trail there'd be no chance at all of catching up with the train tonight. Maybe they'd *never* catch up!

He shook his head. Pa seemed disappointed. "I was hopin' you could be of some help," was all he said. It made Jason feel worse than a real scolding.

Just then Scout started down one of the paths, barking. He looked back at them, then ran on.

"Pa, that's the way to go! Scout knows!"

"Pshaw! That dog isn't smart enough to—"

"He *is*, Pa! He can smell those wagon tracks, I bet. Mebbe that sorrel of McDermott's, too!"

Pa hesitated, then shrugged. "Get back in the wagon, then. Get him back, too. We'll see where he takes us. But if he's wrong . . ."

Jason didn't wait for his father to finish. He whistled for Scout.

A quarter moon, bright as a new penny, was beginning to show in the sky.

They had gone only a few more miles when Jason smelled wood smoke. He saw the red glare of a camp fire ahead and heard the high, shrill whinny of a horse.

"Pa! It's the train!"

"So it is, son!" Pa slapped the reins hard. "Mary, we've caught up with 'em!"

81

"Glory be!" cried Ma.

They all laughed like crazy, which made Scout bark and carry on, too. Jason could hardly hold him.

McDermott was the first to hurry to meet them. "Bartow! I've been watchin' for ye! Did you find your little gal?" He spied Abbie then and gave a whoop like an Indian war call.

They all got down from the wagon, McDermott lifting Abbie gently, as if he thought she might break.

Folks crowded around. The men thumped Pa on the back. The women hugged Ma and fussed over Abbie. Everybody talked at once.

"Who found her, you say?" somebody asked again.

"Why, the boy did," Pa said, and put his hand on Jason's shoulder.

"No, Pa. It wasn't me. It was *him*." Jason pointed to Scout, sitting quietly, head to one side. "Remember?"

"Oh, yes," said Pa, as if it didn't matter. He went on talking.

Jason's mouth hung open. Pa wasn't going to give Scout credit for finding Abbie! Nor for setting them on the right trail, either. He stooped down and rubbed the dog's ears. "It isn't fair!" he whispered. "It just isn't *fair*!"

15

Two days later they arrived at Fort Laramie. "Not a bit too soon," Ma said. "We're out of flour, beans, coffee—most everything."

Jason's heart sank as they pulled up to the gate. He looked at the fort listlessly, not much caring what it was like. The walls were about fifteen feet high, and had wooden spikes on top. At each corner was a sort of tower where a sentry stood guard.

Then Jason saw the Indians. He sat up straight. They were hanging around outside the gate, wanting to get in. Did the sentry know? Jason wondered. He moved closer to Pa on the front seat, pointing to them.

"They won't bother us none," Pa said. "Mac told me about 'em. They're the friendly kind. All they want is a chance to barter—horses, pelts, leather goods they make—for other supplies."

Pa told him, too, what McDermott had said about Laramie. The U.S. government had made it a military post just last year, in 1849. It was supposed to be a help to folks like themselves, crossing the Wyoming Territory.

Pa's wagon was in line to be first through the gate. "The rest of you wait here," McDermott yelled. "Bartow an' me, we'll go see the officer in charge and find out where he aims to quarter us."

Once they were inside the fort, Pa handed the reins to Jason. McDermott tied his horse to a hitching rail. The two men stomped up wooden steps and disappeared into a building.

"Mercy, it's hot!" Ma exclaimed, wiping Abbie's flushed face with the corner of her apron. "I hope they won't be long."

Jason looked around. The fort was sure a busy place. Men in blue uniforms were everywhere. Some marched up and down briskly, drilling. Others worked at currying horses, waxing saddles, or cleaning rifles. He could hear the sharp clang of a blacksmith's anvil. He caught the yeasty smell of fresh bread baking, too.

Women wearing calico dresses and sunbonnets like Ma's walked past, some with children clinging to their skirts. They nodded and smiled.

A couple of mangy dogs ran up to the wagon. Scout's hair bristled. He growled a warning, even though they were bigger than he was. They went on.

An American flag hung proudly from a tall pole in the middle of the fort. Next to that was a well that everybody in the fort used. Jason watched a boy about his own age, in buckskin breeches, draw up a bucket of water and stagger off with it.

"Why doesn't Pa come?" Abbie asked.

Jason hoped that Pa and McDermott would talk to the commander a long time. It gave him that much longer with

Scout. Because as soon as things were settled in there and Pa came out . . .

Just then a corporal sauntered up—a young fellow with a moustache like a piece of straw under his sunburned nose. He tipped his hat to Ma politely. "Where you folks from, ma'am?" he asked.

"Pennsylvania," Ma said. "We're bound for Oregon. But, I declare, I wonder if we'll ever get there."

"It's a long ways," the corporal agreed. "You'll likely be on the trail three more months, mebbe longer." He reached out to pet Scout, who was sitting on the front seat, and Scout didn't mind. "That's a fine dog you've got," he said. He looked at Jason. "Is he yours?"

"Yes, sir," Jason said quickly.

"You know, he's the spittin' image of another dog I saw." The soldier scratched Scout under the chin. "Fact is, if I didn't know better I'd swear he was the one Mrs. Morris just lost."

"Well, he *isn't*," Jason said indignantly and jerked Scout away.

But Ma asked, "Mrs. Morris? Who might she be?"

"Why, she's the wife of our new commanding officer. A mighty nice lady. She just got here a week or so ago." The corporal rested one shiny boot against the hub of the wagon's front wheel. "Seems she lost this dog of hers on the way out here. She's still upset. Can't get over it." He shook his head. "Looked just like this."

"How do *you* know what her dog looked like? Did you see it?" Jason blurted out. Ma nudged him in the ribs and he knew he shouldn't have said that.

"Well, I didn't exactly see it." The young fellow hesitated.

"I saw a picture of it, though." He smoothed the sparse hair of his moustache. "Y'see, I was in charge of the work party that moved the commander into his quarters. We were opening some boxes and we came across this drawing some artist fellow made. 'That's my dog,' Mrs. Morris told us." The corporal kicked at the wagon's hub. " 'Only I lost him,' she said. I could tell she felt real bad."

"Oh, the poor soul!" Ma looked right at Jason.

Pa came out of the commander's office then and strode over. "This is my husband, Mr. Bartow," Ma said. She turned to Pa. "Henry, this young fellow says Scout resembles a dog the commander's wife lost."

"That so? Where did she lose it?" Pa asked.

"In Missouri," the corporal answered. "Independence, I think she said."

"Why, that's where we got Scout!" Abbie cried. She had been listening, openmouthed, to every word. "He got *us*, though. He was a stray. He followed Jason and—"

"Shut up, *you!*" Jason lashed out at her.

"Watch your tongue, boy!" Pa glared at him.

"Well, I didn't mean to cause you trouble . . ." The corporal was backing away, embarrassed. "I'm probably talking foolish. Not likely it's the same dog."

"We'll soon find out," Pa said, and touched his fingers to the brim of his hat. "Much obliged for tellin' us. Now would you be so good as to point out the commander's quarters for me?"

When the corporal had gone, Pa said, "We'll go right now. Give the dog to this Mrs. Morris. That is, if he's rightfully hers." His jaw was set like it always was when his mind was made up.

"He isn't hers, Pa! That soldier doesn't know for sure. He

said so himself. Scout's *mine* and I aim to . . ." the words choked in his throat.

"But Jason . . ." Ma's touch was light on his shoulder. "You can't keep him if he belongs to somebody else." She looked at Scout wistfully. "Goodness knows I'll miss him. But when I think of that poor woman's heartache . . ." She threw up her hands. "It's the only kind thing to do. You can understand that, can't you?"

Jason didn't answer. He couldn't say what he was thinking— that he *hated* the commander's wife. He hated that corporal, too, for sticking his nose into other folks' affairs. And he almost hated Abbie. Her and her silly babbling!

They all climbed down from the wagon and followed Pa, as he ordered. Jason dragged behind, clutching Scout to his chest. Every step that brought him nearer to the commander's wife made the ache inside him bigger.

They came to a small wooden house. It was like the others beside it, except that it had a porch with three steps. They went slowly up them. Pa rapped on the door.

Jason hung back and Ma pushed him forward gently. "Now, don't take it so hard. We'll get you another dog, once we're settled in Oregon."

"I don't want another dog!" He jerked away, his eyes smarting. "I don't *ever* want another dog if I can't have Scout!"

"Yes?" A pretty woman opened the door. She had a knot of honey-colored hair at her neck, and soft curls framed her face.

Pa took off his hat. "Mrs. Morris? We heard you lost a dog back in Independence." He pointed to Scout. "Could this be the one?"

The commander's wife came closer. When she was near Jason could smell something like flowers—roses, maybe.

87

"Why, it is!" she cried. "It's my Jimbo!" She reached for him.

Jason glared at her. He held Scout as tight as he could. He could feel the dog's heart beat against his own.

"Give him to her, son," Pa said.

Jason swallowed hard. Slowly, he handed Scout over. He felt as though a part of himself was being torn away.

The woman hugged Scout and fussed over him, calling him silly, sweet names. Scout seemed to like her. His tail was going and he tried to kiss her cheek.

"How can I ever thank you for bringing him back to me?" Mrs. Morris smiled at Jason, but he looked away.

"I know how you must have missed him," Ma said.

And Pa added, "We're mighty glad the dog's found his rightful home. Aren't we, Jason?"

Jason didn't answer. He started down the steps fast. He had to get out of there. He couldn't stand to see Scout and the woman so happy together. Not when he . . .

Just then Scout leaped from the woman's arms and came after him, whimpering. Mrs. Morris hurried to snatch Scout up. "Are you trying to run away again, Jimbo?" she scolded. "I guess I'll have to keep you tied up from now on." She brushed at a brown spot on Scout's head, then frowned. "Wait a minute. My dog didn't have a mark like this!" She looked puzzled. "Why, I don't believe you're Jimbo after all! Your ears are longer and . . ."

"You're sure, ma'am?" Pa asked.

She nodded. Her face had been shining like the candles on a Christmas tree, but now the candles were all out. "He's so much like my dog, I wanted to think . . ." Her voice trembled.

Jason held his breath. *Now Pa's going to tell her she can*

have him anyway, if she wants. He's been meaning to get rid of him. Here's his chance.

He and Pa looked at each other for a long minute.

Pa cleared his throat with a rasping sound. "Well, I reckon my boy'll keep him, then."

Jason stared. He couldn't believe what he had heard. "You mean . . . ?"

Pa kept on talking to Mrs. Morris. "Him and that dog are mighty close. They've been through a lot together. They'll be through a lot more before we get where we're goin'. It won't matter, though, long as they've got each other. Right, Jason?"

Jason could only nod. A warm feeling came over him. Pa *did* understand, then. He'd probably always understood. Only he wasn't the kind to listen to his heart instead of his head. That didn't mean he didn't have plenty of love to share. I'll have to remember that from now on, Jason thought.

Mrs. Morris was looking at Jason. Her eyes were the prettiest he'd ever seen, soft and brown. They were kind of misty, though. She gave Scout a final pat. "I can tell you care for him very much," she said. "I just hope someone like you will find *my* dog, wherever he is."

Ma reached out and gave the woman's hand a little squeeze. Pa twisted his hat, anxious to be going. They walked away, Abbie turning and waving.

"Good-bye," Jason said.

Scout trotted to the wagon beside him, tail swinging, lifting his feet high. Like me and him own the whole world, Jason thought.

They were leaving Fort Laramie. After a week's stay there they were ready to tackle the snowcapped Rockies McDermott talked so much about.

Now everyone had a good supply of food. The horses had been re-shod. Some of the oxen with sore, cracked hooves had had them scraped and cleaned with lye. Pa had a new wooden tongue made for the front axle of the wagon and some extra linchpins to hold the wheels on, in case theirs broke.

The doctor at the fort had warned about an epidemic of cholera spreading eastward from the Rockies. He'd stocked folks with Paynter's Cure, which would help some if they took sick.

As the gates swung open, McDermott rode up. He tossed something and Jason caught it. It was a braided loop of rawhide, fancy with red and yellow beads.

"Try *that* on your dog for size!" McDermott was grinning through his beard. "Had an Indian make it for 'im."

The mountain man was gone to the head of the train before Jason could open his mouth.

Jason fastened the collar about Scout's neck. It fit perfectly.

"Look, Pa."

"That'll do fine until we get to Oregon," Pa said. "Then he'll likely need a bigger one."

"Roll . . . out!" McDermott boomed.

The oxen, slow and clumsy, began to pull the wagon. Everyone waved good-bye. The soldiers stood at attention, saluting.

"We're goin' West, you an' me!" Jason put his arm around Scout and held him tight. "*West!* You hear?"